LORD AGRAVAINE LOST...

Old things dwell in the forest. Older than cities and older than roads. Older even than the coming of humans. The forest is home to many things that have no name, for never have mortal eyes been laid upon them.

Within the darkness of the woods, these old things abide. They are neither friendly nor foes; they are not bound by such distinctions…

Lord Agravaine gazed upon them now, his head resting on the trunk of a towering ash, his eyes open wide. The things of the deep forest watched him…

They even pricked a drop or two of blood for their tinctures…

Great Fantasy from PHOENIX AND FOX EMPORIUM

☐ **ELLIPSES by Jerry Patchett** (125746 -- $2.95)*

☐ **GAGMOG AND HELEN by Richard Silverfish** (139925 -- $2.25)*

☐ **TREES WITHIN THE FOREST by Joseph Pesci** (086147 -- $1.95)*

☐ **THE WITCH OF THORNWILLOW by Wren Feeney** (115299 -- $2.50)*

☐ **GLASS ONION by Jon Vigi** (090327 -- $2.25)*

☐ **THE DINOSAUR CONUNDRUM by Michael Pesci** (147492 -- $2.25)*

☐ **JASON THE MEGATHERIUM by The Funcle** (611785 -- $2.50)*

☐ **SANCTUARY FOR ELEPHANTS by V.G.C. Mona** (135388 -- $1.75)*

☐ **MAGES: Jacob Ustikoff's Wondrous Worlds of Fantasy #1 edited by Vin Cartier and L. Spaulding DeCarp** (125771 -- $3.50)*

☐ **KEEPER OF SECRETS AND HALF-TRUTHS by Katherine Shipman** (064912 -- $2.50)*

☐ **SHADOWS OF THE REPUBLIC by Marcus Skywalker** (097825 -- $2.50)*

☐ **LADY TYGER by Juan Phillips Armstrong** (306011-- $2.75)*

☐ **WINSTON'S WORLD by Dan Vigi** (217741-- $2.25)*

*Prices slightly higher in Canada.

Buy them at your local bookstore or use this coupon for ordering.

THE NEW FICTIONAL LIBRARY, INC.
P.O. BOX 000, Greenhouse, Michigan 02021

Please send me the books I have checked above. I am enclosing $________________
(please add $1.00 to this order to cover postage and handling). Send check or money order -- no cash or C.O.D.'s. Prices and numbers are subject to change without notice.

Name____

Address____

City____________________________ State________________ Zip Code____________

Allow 4-6 weeks for delivery.
This offer is fake; please do not send money.

A.R. RATHMANN

Gates to Illvelion

A Phoenix and Fox Emporium Fantasy

Gates to Illvelion
Copyright 2023 by A.R. Rathmann

Printed in the United States of America
Published in 2023 by Phoenix and Fox Emporium
First paperback edition, 2023

Phoenix and Fox Emporium
www.phoenixandfoxemporium.com

Cover Design by Matsya Das
https://www.matsyadas.com/

Gates to Illvelion/A.R. Rathmann — 1st ed.
Paperback ISBN: 978-1-959362-00-5

A.R. RATHMANN

Gates to Illvelion

A looking-glass shows two reflections: the face we cannot see and the face we can.

— WISDOM FROM OLD ESTLINE

GATES TO ILLVELION

CHAPTER ONE

FAERIE NIGHT

Gwenhivar's dress was the color of sapphires. She had worn it especially for this night, for the dancing and revelry that their twilight escapade promised. Her first faerie reel.

She hoped the blue coloring of her bodice and skirt would gleam in the moonlight, would shimmer as she spun around the circle and kicked up her heels. Her father had said the dancing could be wild and unrestrained. Gwenhivar longed to take off her slippers and let her toes spread out amongst the wet grass.

Her father, Lord Agravaine of Estline, had been to the faerie reel many times, but this was the first time he'd allowed his young daughter to come, the first time he'd even spoken to her of what it entailed.

"You must be willing to dance freely. No restraint. No decorum. It is a night for abandon." His grey eyes smiled at her, the skin around them crinkling with affection. Though he tried to keep his lips straight and his face serious, the joy in his eyes betrayed him. He wanted her to have a good time.

"There aren't really fairies in the forest are there, Father?" Gwenhivar's voice was like a tinkling bell. She put her thin fingers into her father's broad hands.

"Who can say?" he returned. "But we dance for their pleasure, for if we do not, they will reap their fury upon us." Agravaine spoke so solemnly that for a moment Gwenhivar almost believed him.

"What a jest you give me, Father!" she laughed.

But the lord Agravaine merely smiled upon his golden-haired daughter and kissed her forehead.

"Just promise me," he said, "you won't go past the edge of the forest."

"I promise. But why?"

This time, the joy in his eyes was gone. "Wild and fearsome things live upon the edges, my love. Do not go too near."

Gwenhivar promised, though, in her heart, she held something back.

They came to the dewy lawn, the sun now almost set and dim twilight descending. Others were gathered on the grass, men and women, old and young, all smiling merrily and chatting in whispers. The sky was pale pink and turning dark fast. Gwenhivar stood on the edge of the gathering, feeling shyer than she had expected. Her father's firm hand squeezed her own.

"Remember, dear Gwen, you must dance with wild abandon."

"Yes, but—"

She had no time to finish. As the last wisps of sunset faded and the stars began to sparkle, the revelers clapped hands, someone rang a bright bell, and the drums beat a heavy rhythm. The dance had begun.

Lord Agravaine smiled once upon his daughter then leapt into the circle. The folks there—who just minutes before had been standing reserved and hushed upon the grass—had thrown off their courtesies and spun like tops. They weaved a circle and raised hands together; they shouted and stamped their feet to the ta-rum, ta-rum, ta-rum of the kettle drum.

Gwenhivar stood apart, her sapphire dress almost as dark as the sky. The moon had not yet come out. She knew she must dance, but now that the moment was upon her, her feet froze.

My feet! she thought. Yes, that would help. Removing her slippers, she let her bare toes sink into the chilled grass. The earth was soft, like flesh, and the grass cooled and tickled her skin. This simple thing, this simple change had lessened the fear within her.

"Come! Come!" the other dancers shouted. The drum beat harder and faster. Gwenhivar looked to the circle, to the reeling dancers, and saw her father, his smile bigger and broader than she had ever seen, as if some great weight had been lifted from his features. He looked like a young man suddenly, almost as young as she.

The first step was the hardest, but then the rhythm of the drums beat itself into her very bones. She learned what it was to let go, to abandon all constraint. Above them, fireflies flitted, and the moon shone like a pale-gray pearl. Gwenhivar danced, her sapphire skirt spreading out around her like rippling waves. She caught sight of her father's face as she spun; he beamed happily, delighting in her unbound joy.

Wild whoops and cries of mirth burst from the dancers' lips. Gwenhivar had no other thought but, *Freedom! Freedom! Freedom!* She felt sweat drip down her face, the heat of her body cooling quickly in the night air.

"Do the fairies see us?" she cried. "Do they approve?" She spoke to no one in particular, just to the air and the wisps of clouds above her head.

"Too close, my love! Too close!"

It was her father's voice. Tense. Fearful.

"The edge!"

Gwenhivar had closed her eyes and spun and stomped with no thought of herself. Her body was but a conduit for the rhythm. She opened her eyes now—as her father was shouting—and saw that she was on the edge of the forest.

The blackness of the woods was all she could see. That blackness, deep and seemingly endless. Trying to lunge back, to return to the circle of dancers, Gwenhivar took an ill-placed step, and she felt her feet give way beneath her. She stumbled.

Into the blackness, into the fortress of trees, she fell.

As soon as it had happened, it was as if a wall had been erected between herself and the revelers. She heard nothing of the drum beats or the shouts. All was silence. All was darkness. She had tumbled into another world.

At first, she was too surprised to feel anything. But then a dread overcame her. Soft but savage chittering could be heard all around as if the creatures of the forest were laughing at her from behind their hidden places. The sounds were inhuman and cruel.

"Who's there?" Gwenhivar shouted. But the chittering voices grew louder, and cackles like the braying of donkeys resounded off the tree trunks.

Though she could not see them, Gwenhivar knew the creatures were scurrying toward her, surrounding her. She felt the rising panic of one caught in a trap.

"Father!" she cried, unsure if anyone outside this darkness could hear her.

The creatures were closing in; teeth glinted in the small patches of moonlight that sifted through the leaves. Sharp and wet with saliva, the grinning teeth were all around her, ready to bite.

Fear swallowed her voice.

"Gwen!" It was her father, crashing through the darkness. The surrounding creatures scattered. "Go! Flee!" Lord Agravaine was pulling at his daughter's arms, grasping at the folds of her dress. Gwenhivar felt the material tear. But Agravaine was like a wild animal, like a madman, trying desperately to pull the girl up and fling her to safety. Gwenhivar tried to run, but something stopped her.

Her foot was caught.

A protruding tree root had somehow enveloped her ankle. She squirmed to wriggle free, but the creatures were returning now, their momentary fright averted.

"Begone!" cried Lord Agravaine. His sword was out now, stinging like a serpent's fang.

The creatures were like a swarm of hornets. They bit and tore and scratched at every part of Agravaine's body. Gwenhivar heard his screams, but she saw little. A cloud of utter darkness had descended upon him.

Tears poured down her face as she tried to free herself, tried to aid her father. But it was no use; the tree root seemed to squeeze her ankle tighter. She clawed at it with her fingers, scratching the skin raw against the rough bark. But the more she clawed, the more tightly the root held fast. Tears and sweat mingled so much in her eyes that her vision blurred. The braying cries of the creatures started to fade as if they were galloping off, escaping further into the heart of the forest.

At last, it was silent. All was still, and Gwenhivar was alone.

Gone were the creatures. Gone was her father. A bright streak of moonlight pierced the trees and showed her the edge of the forest. There—beckoning her—were the other revelers.

"Come!" they all called. "Come out of the forest! Quick!"

Beyond the trees was the dewy lawn, the soft, cool soil. She caught a glimpse of her shoes, resting placidly on the grass. Gwenhivar couldn't help but laugh bitterly. As ordinary as anything, her silken shoes lay there, a reminder of the laughter and dancing that had only been happening moments before.

Before she had fallen past the edge of the forest.

She saw the desperate, pleading eyes of the others, but she could not answer them.

"Come!" they said. "Quick, before the fairies return!"

But how could she leave the forest now? Her father was within, taken away by its wicked denizens. She could not leave him. Somehow, Gwenhivar knew her father was still alive.

The root relaxed its grip, and standing upon bare feet, Gwenhivar raised a parting farewell to the onlookers beyond the edge of the forest.

Then she bounded off, heading deeper into the dark woods.

CHAPTER TWO

A HEART WROUGHT WITH SPELLS

Old things dwell in the forest. Older than cities and older than roads. Older even than the coming of humans. The forest is home to many things that have no name, for never have mortal eyes been laid upon them. Within the darkness of the woods, these old things abide. They are neither friendly nor foes; they are not bound by such distinctions.

Things of moss and flower, things of stone and mud. Things of earth and air. Deep within the forest. They dwell and they abide, and few mortal eyes look upon them.

Lord Agravaine gazed upon them now, his head resting on the trunk of a towering ash, his eyes open wide. The things of the deep forest watched him, snatching some threads from his clothes, plucking some strands of his hair. They even pricked a drop of blood or two for their tinctures.

Agravaine made no movements to stop them. He stared blankly as one made dumb by some spell. Indeed, he was bewitched. The fairies had seen to it when they carried him off. But for what purpose or to what end, Agravaine did not know. He knew nothing, other than he was a warm body resting peacefully beside the ash tree. He cared not for his fate or his future. He was content in his enchantment. He was a happy spectacle to the deep things in the dark woods.

Older than anything human, the things of the forest slowly made feast upon the man who had been delivered into their midst.

❧

At first, it looked like a great big pile of leaves, but as Gwenhivar stepped closer, she considered that perhaps it was something more. A kind of nest, perhaps. Or a hovel, or even a cave. But something about it seemed strange. The strangest thing she had seen since running off into the forest.

When she had first run off, she had no idea which way to go or what paths to follow. She saw no trail and heard no sound. All was twilight gloom, though the moon peeked through the treetops and gave some small streams of illumination to guide her. The forest had been eerily quiet, unnaturally still. Without direction or track to follow, she had headed toward the center of the woods. For what seemed like hours, Gwenhivar had stumbled and trudged through the brambles and trees, with no sign of her father or the fairies. Despair had begun to set in, a dreadful panic that made her imagination run wild. The darkness made it worse, and she realized the foolishness of what she had done.

What if she were to be lost and trapped in the forest forever? What if she wandered endlessly without ever seeing her father? What if she were captured too and tortured by hideous monsters, monsters worse than even the fairies?

The painful dread of these thoughts was almost too much to bear, so Gwenhivar forced them from her mind. She kept moving her feet, one in front of the other, taking care not to step on sharp rocks or nettles. Her bare feet were becoming dust-covered: an earthy brown, like the soil she walked upon. Her toenails were lined with dirt, and the soles of her feet ached with weariness. Still, she had marched on. And still, the moon had given her some light with which to see.

It was when the weariness had almost consumed her that she came upon the pit of leaves. Wider than a span of ten horses, taller than her head, the pile was bathed in moonlight. The silver light gleamed atop the leaves as if pointing to a sign. Gwenhivar had stared at it for several long minutes, trying to puzzle out what made it seem so strange. After waiting and watching, all she could think was that this huge mound of leaves was some kind of dwelling. But what dwelled within, she was afraid to think.

Utter exhaustion came upon her suddenly, and she felt every bone in her body ache. She needed to rest, needed to sleep, but the thought of sleeping in this forest with nothing to guard her and nothing to hide her was almost too terrifying to contemplate. Perhaps if she nestled on the edge of the leaf mound she might use it for some cover.

Her eyes were too heavy to keep open now, and despite her misgivings, she gave in to drowsy sleep. Curling up beside the leaf pile, she made herself as small as she could and using some stray leaves for a pillow, she fell into a deep and dreamless sleep.

The next thing she knew, she was waking to the warm and yellow light of the sunrise. She stretched and rubbed the sleep from her eyes. Her body still ached, and her sapphire dress was wrinkled and covered with bits of crumpled leaves, but at least she had slept, and at least it was morning. Nothing had accosted her in the night. As she sat up and stretched her arms once more, she blinked, shaking the last remaining flakes of slumber from her eyes.

It was then that she saw the Thing. "What acorn has fallen here?" it said.

Towering over Gwenhivar, the Thing looked as if a barrel full of leaves had detached itself from the mound and come to life. Hulking and shaggy, it had a nose like a protruding mushroom and eyes as beady as a squirrel's. The mouth was a gaping, blackened maw; Gwenhivar thought it seemed rather like looking down the hollow of a huge tree. But the voice was most unsettling. High and nasal, it sounded like the screech of a nagging fisherman's wife.

"Or not an acorn but a bright blue star," the Thing said, bending down with leafy, dirty fingers to paw at Gwenhivar's skirt.

The girl shrank from the Thing's touch, scampering to her feet and backing away. She wondered if she could flee or if the creature moved faster than it looked.

"Don't be afeared now," the Thing continued, not the least bit offended by Gwen's fright. "Old Troll-Hag shan't be hurting. Though I do look a sight, I'm sure. Human eyes ain't set their sights on me in many an age. Why came ye here, child?" The creature called Troll-Hag smiled: a toothless thing, though not, to Gwen's surprise, unfriendly.

"I- I am called Gwenhivar," she stammered.

"Aye, and what be yer business?"

"My father. He was taken by the fairies."

A look of understanding passed over Troll-Hag's dirt-and-leaf-covered face. She nodded matter-of-factly then held out her arm toward the vast mound of leaves. "Come then, child. Into my abode and we'll see what's to be done."

It was as if a trick had been played upon Gwenhivar's eyes, for where once she had only seen a vast mound of leaves there now appeared a wooden door, which led into the leafy hovel.

Troll-Hag knocked three times and the door swung open of its own accord. "In ye go!" said Troll-Hag, moving quickly and ushering Gwen through the portal. In she went without even a chance to protest, while the massive body of Troll-Hag followed close behind, making sure to block the way out with her massive girth.

The door shut with a heavy thud.

Inside, the hovel was not at all what Gwenhivar had expected.

Perhaps she figured it would be damp and musty and soil-like, as if the lair of a beetle had been expanded to great size. But instead, it was warm and bathed in a glow of yellow light, and all around, shelves upon shelves lined the walls, and upon those shelves were dozens and dozens of bric-a-brac and baubles, all of them piled up together on the teetering shelves, giving Gwen the feeling she had entered the confines of a very cluttered curiosity shop.

There were pieces of crockery and stopped clocks and shimmering figurines all made of glass; and watch chains and leather shoes and telescopes; and feather quills and rolls of parchment and porcelain dolls wearing smudged dresses. On and on and on the junk went, a dizzying display of forgotten treasures.

In the very center of the room were a simple round table, a stool, and an immense rocking chair made of what Gwenhivar could only describe as sculpted moss. Toadstools and other fungi sprouted along the dirt floor like a living carpet.

"There's only the stool to sit upon," said Troll-Hag as she happily flopped into her seat in the rocking chair. She waved to the short stool and Gwenhivar took a seat. Gwen's lowly position only made the massive form of Troll-Hag loom larger as she sat in her moss chair and frowned slightly at the girl.

"Looking for yer father, eh?"

"Yes."

Troll-Hag grunted. "Haven't found him?"

"No, ma'am."

"As to be expected."

"But why!" Gwen didn't mean to shout, but her frustration, discomfort, and panic were rising. She felt suddenly like this was a dangerous delay, an unwelcome waste of time.

"Got no magic in ye, that's why." Troll-Hag said this matter-of-factly, as if Gwen should've known. "No magic. And that's why all ye've found is dirt and trees and nary a Faerie creature at all."

"I found you," answered Gwen, defiantly.

Troll-Hag scoffed. "Bah! I'm half dirt and leaves! Why do ye think I have all these silly trinkets?" She waved her massive hands at the shelves. "Wanderers and lovers and curious folk all stumble upon my mound eventually. I don't make myself known, of course, but they find this place nonetheless. And they're forever losing things! Should think ye humans would take more care of yer treasures."

Gwenhivar had no treasures to lose. Her only finery was her dress, but even that looked worse for wear after so many hours wandering and sleeping among the leaves.

"So it is hopeless, then?" asked the girl. "I will never find my father?" The words hurt Gwen's throat as she said them. The doom of being an orphan choked her.

Troll-Hag clucked her tongue and shook her head. "Leave it to youth to jump to conclusions! Did I say 'hopeless,' child? I said ye had no magic. To find anything at all in these woods, ye must have a spell put inside ye."

Gwenhivar didn't quite understand, and she disliked the implications.

"Don't give me that look, child!" said Troll-Hag. "I don't make these rules. Have no control over them whatsoever. But they be the rules, and thee must abide. Now, what to do for the spell…"

The creature pulled herself up out of her chair and shuffled over to one of the cluttered shelves. With a thick, long finger, she pointed from trinket to trinket, mumbling as she went. "Too sharp, too sharp," she muttered, then, "A bit dingy, that one. No good," then, "Too new," and, "Too kind," and, "Too wet."

Troll-Hag circled the large room thrice, until at last she shook her head, returned to the moss chair, and sank into it in defeat.

"What's the matter?" asked Gwenhivar.

"Nothing doing, I'm afeared. Not a single thing is right for the spell."

"Why do we need a thing? And now that we're on the subject again, I'm not quite sure I want to have a spell put on me at all."

"Not *on* thee, dearie. *In* thee. And we need a thing to make the spell. I can't just wave a hand and make it. It must be made with a thing, and when we've made the spell, then ye must swallow it. And when ye have swallowed it, ye shall have the spell inside thee. And then—" Troll-Hag's dark eyes brightened "—ye'll find what it is ye seek."

"Why are all these things upon the shelves wrong for the spell? Surely you could cook a stew or broth and put the spell in that?"

"Bah! Stews ain't right for the spell, child! A spell needs something of worth. Something right."

"Yes, but—" Gwen did not finish. She watched as Troll-Hag's eyes stared intently at the skirt of her sapphire dress. Troll-Hag's mouth slackened as she fell into a silent daze.

"By stick and by stone," she murmured. "The very dust of twilight." She stood up from her chair and reached a hand toward Gwen's skirt. "That'll do indeed."

Gwenhivar couldn't help but laugh. "I'm not going to eat my dress if that's what you think!"

"Eh? No, child, what do ye take me for? Eating dresses is absurd. But—" she fingered the shimmering material in her thick hand "—the dust of twilight is another matter."

The next thing Gwen knew, Troll-Hag had grabbed a dull kitchen knife and a clay bowl from one of her shelves, and while holding the folds of the dress over the bowl, she began scraping the surface of it with the knife. In amazement, Gwen watched as tiny particles of glimmering blue fluttered down into the bowl.

As Troll-Hag scraped, the color of the dress faded, like stars twinkling out at first light of dawn. The bowl filled with sapphire. When she was finished, Troll-Hag whisked away the bowl and set it on the wooden table. She stirred it with her heavy finger and mumbled such words as Gwen could not understand. Then she turned and held the bowl under the girl's chin.

"Here 'tis, child. The spell."

"Am I supposed to swallow it?" Gwenhivar shrank from the fine blue dust beneath her nose.

"Shall I cut thee open then and put it next to yer heart? Of course, ye must swallow!"

"I shall choke or gag at the very least."

Troll-Hag sighed and shook her head. "Ye humans be so delicate. No wonder ye break and bleed with ease." She grabbed a pitcher from a shelf and poured clear rainwater into the bowl. The specks of sapphire swirled like the heavens.

Hesitantly, Gwenhivar took the bowl in her hands and lifted it to her lips. The water was surprisingly cool, and she neither felt nor tasted the tiny particles of stardust. Instead, what she tasted was Night itself: that cold quality of night that one feels in the air when the sun has set and warmth has gone out of the earth.

Gwen didn't even shiver, though. This wasn't a cold put upon her to make her skin prickle; this was a cold within her that dulled everything, even her heart.

"There," said Troll-Hag, "the change has come. You have it inside you now."

"I feel..." Gwenhivar couldn't articulate it. "It's like I've lost something."

"That's to be expected. Yer heart is wreathed now with a spell. And when a human's heart is thus wrought, she is but a little less human."

Gwenhivar felt goosebumps prickle across her skin. Her throat tightened. "What will happen to me? Can the spell be removed?"

"Aye, it can," answered Troll-Hag. "But then ye'll never find yer father."

Gwen tried to swallow her fear, but it stuck fast in the back of her throat like a fishbone. "What does it mean to be 'a little less human'? Will I—" Gwen hesitated. She stared at Troll-Hag and grimaced, imagining herself becoming something as strange and hideous as this leafy creature before her.

Troll-Hag caught the look and pursed her lips.

"I mean to say," Gwen began again, embarrassed, "will my appearance change?"

"Thinking ye may sprout twigs from yer ears and grow a toadstool nose, eh?" Troll-Hag chuckled at the frightened girl's vanity. "I can't rightly say, but I doubt it. Perhaps yer skin may turn a sickly green?"

Troll-Hag continued to chuckle, and Gwen suspected she was teasing. But still, she felt her stomach lurch at the thought of such changes or worse.

"Indeed ye shall change," Troll-Hag continued, her smile fading. "That much is sure. As sure as the sun and the moon and the stars which ye have now consumed."

Gwen thought of her father. *What would he say of these changes, if he saw them?* But as Gwen started to think of Lord Agravaine, she found that it was hard to remember certain things. She could picture his face clearly enough—the dark hair, the laughing wrinkles around his eyes, the sorrow that passed over his face when he mentioned Gwen's mother—but there were other parts of her father that Gwen could not remember, other things which seemed hidden by some strange darkness. As she struggled to remember, as she searched the corners of her mind, she knew she should be worried.

And yet she wasn't.

The memories of her father were seemingly gone, and yet Gwenhivar was not disturbed by their departure. She had a faint sense of missing them, like one who misses sight of a great eagle flying overhead, but she was not upset. The memories were now faint echoes, blurred outlines of what had once been. She couldn't recall the details of them even as she knew they were missing. The sound of his voice when he used to sing her to sleep, the firmness and warmth of his hand when he held her own, the stories they told each other as they sat by the fire at night, the joy of harvest time when Agravaine took up the scythe and helped his tenants gather in the wheat: all of these Gwenhivar knew had happened, and yet she felt nothing for them. They were like tales read in a book, both real and unreal, but they did not touch her heart.

She said none of this to Troll-Hag. Instead, she nodded and thanked the creature. "What is done cannot be undone. As you say, now I can find my father."

"Aye, indeed."

"When I leave this hut, what will I see outside in

the woods? Will the path be laid clear?" Gwen knew the answer already, but still, she asked.

Troll-Hag shook her head. "'Tis no path. But yer eyes'll be open now to that which is of Faerie."

"Then I thank you," she said and curtsied to the creature. The hem of her beautiful sapphire dress was now faded gray and dull like a pile of ashes. "If I shall find my way here again, my father and I will give you reward."

"No need for that, child! Troll-Hag is always happy to be of service." Troll-Hag grinned and the leaves around her mouth rustled and shivered.

When Gwen stepped outside, the hovel of leaves and the creature and everything within disappeared. What stood in its place was a man, tall and regal, and covered in blood.

CHAPTER THREE

GWENHIVAR'S CHOICE

To Gwen's puzzlement, she wasn't frightened or shocked by the man. There was that coldness again, that sunless chill that welled up inside her.

The man, for his part, seemed unperturbed as well, despite the blood which soaked his doublet.

The two stared at one another for a long moment. At last, the man opened his mouth to speak but the sound that came forth was a kind of screech, like an eagle's cry. And then he dropped to the ground, grasping his throat and writhing like a wounded snake.

As he struggled upon the ground, all Gwenhivar could think was that perhaps his face looked familiar. *Is he my father?* she thought. She knew in an instant that such a thought was ridiculous, but the fact that she could think it at all disturbed her. Her father looked nothing like this strange dying man.

At last, he stopped moving. Sudden regret and shame welled up within the girl as she realized she had done nothing but stare as he had fallen to his death. But her guilt dissipated almost as quickly as it arose because the man upon the ground began to change: his body turned to wet soil and brown earth, then grass took to seed and sprouted up all over him, and soon flowers too, and not a moment later the man was gone, transformed into a mound of cornflower and primrose and yarrow. It was as if a decade had passed in the span of a minute, the whole cycle of decay and decomposition and regrowth and renewal altogether in one sudden flash.

While she stared at the miracle (or, one might say, the unsettling magic), Gwen realized that once again she was not alone. From out of the corners of the surrounding trees came many a strange creature to inspect the newly formed mound. Gwen stepped back quickly and tried to evade the creatures, for they were like nothing she had ever seen before.

A small dog with a squirrel's head, a roe deer with the face of a fox, a raven with paws, and a salamander with wings: all of these and more came creeping towards the mound. Gwen saw a snail as large as a wolfhound and hazel-skinned little people with long noses and bulbous noses and yellow eyes like bile. All of them came towards the flowers and wild grass that had been newly born from the body of the man, and like guests at a feast, they began to munch upon the leaves and petals and stems.

To her surprise, Gwen was not afraid. The creatures seemed harmless and much more interested in eating plants than young girls.

"Excuse me?" she said, stepping forward.

Several creatures stopped and looked up, startled by her presence. They said nothing, however, and Gwen wondered if she could speak their language or if they could speak hers.

"That is to say," she continued, "what just happened? Who was that man?"

The squirrel-headed dog sat on its hind legs and cocked its head. "A faerie knight, of course," it said quickly, speaking just as one would expect a squirrel to speak.

"Aye, aye," echoed the raven.

"A faerie knight?" the girl asked.

"Made by the queen," returned the squirrel, nodding his head at the mound.

"The *queens*," said the roe deer in its smooth, foxy voice. "There are three of them."

"No, no, no! Just one!" insisted the squirrel-dog.

"There's lots and lots, not just three!" squeaked one of the little people whose nose was as long and skinny as a carrot.

The fox-headed deer snarled. "That's impossible. Why would there be more than three?"

"Why would there be three at all?" cried the squirrel, baring its teeth. "There's only one queen, I tell you!"

The snail lurched between the other creatures to calm things. Its mucous-dripping feelers swayed back and forth as if to push the others apart.

"The truth is, none of us knows," said the raven, at last.

"How do you know there is any queen at all?" Gwenhivar asked.

This proposition filled all the creatures with revulsion. They couldn't even find words with which to repel such blasphemies. The snail managed to shake its heavy, viscous head.

"But why should a faerie knight, as you call him, turn into a mound of flowers?" continued Gwen.

"The queen made him so," said the squirrel-dog. "She makes all her faerie knights as such. Tree branches, flowers, rocks, toadstools, sometimes even clumps of brown earth. Mashes them together and makes a knight."

"Yes, but why? And how could he bleed if he's only made of dirt and sticks?"

"Why shouldn't he bleed?" said the roe deer. "If he was alive then he could surely bleed."

Gwenhivar wasn't convinced, but she didn't feel like arguing. "Do all these faerie knights bleed and collapse and turn into vegetation?"

The creatures thought for a moment. At last, the fox-headed deer answered. "I suppose so. They are never quite right, I believe. They don't last."

"You ask an awful lot of questions," the squirrel-dog complained. "And a human too!"

"Yes, a human," echoed the raven. "Why are you in these woods? Unless you have some magic in you?"

"I do," said Gwen firmly. "But I'm not here on holiday if that's what you imply. I'm looking for my father." Her eyes fell upon the flowered mound again. *No*, she thought, *that was not my father.*

"Is he dead too?" asked the squirrel-dog.

"I hope not."

"Hopes are misplaced here," said one of the sallow-faced little men. This one's nose was crooked and had moss growing out of it.

"I must find him," said Gwen, her temper beginning to rise. Her quest would not be quashed by these silly, strange creatures. "Do you have some idea where I might look? To whom I might get help?"

All the creatures looked at one another. Their faces told the same answer.

"The queens, of course," said the roe deer at last.

The squirrel-dog scowled and yelped a bit at this and almost protested again that there was only one queen, but Gwenhivar interrupted. "Where can I find them or her or whomever it is you're talking about?"

Once again, the menagerie looked at one another. All seemed bemused.

"We don't know," a few of them admitted in unison. "We've never seen her."

"Then how do you know—" Gwen stopped herself. She realized this was getting her nowhere, and she'd do better to seek her fortunes elsewhere. Turning to leave, she bowed a little to the strange creatures, thinking that perhaps this was the polite thing to do. But the creatures had already returned to their meal of cornflowers and yarrow and grass.

She walked a short way, moving in a direction that seemed less crowded with trees and brambles when suddenly a hushed voice hissed at her.

"Human!" whispered the voice. "Come here! I know the queen and can take you to her."

Gwen looked around to see who had spoken and saw a small figure, less than her own height, hiding behind a tree. He peeked his head out briefly, and Gwen was startled to see that he was a human too. Sandy-haired and narrow of face, he was dressed in burlap and rags and wore a hat much like the ones the little hazel-skinned people had worn. But though he looked like one of those strange people in dress and manner, he was wholly like Gwen in his bodily appearance.

Gwen made her way toward the boy, and he ventured to come out from behind the tree.

"Why do you hide?" she asked.

"The others. I don't want them to see."

"Because you're human?"

The boy's face stormed with rage. "I'm not! I'm a puck!"

"Well, you look human."

Now the boy's face reddened. "I've been cursed."

Gwen raised an eyebrow.

"I have!" the boy insisted.

"Then why do you hide? Is your curse contagious?"

"'Tis not, but still…" his eyes looked down. "I'm on my own, that's all."

Something about the boy made Gwen feel both pity and tenderness. He was like a lost kitten or a bird with a broken wing. She smiled. "I'm on my own too. Perhaps that makes us perfect companions."

Looking up, the boy's eyes gleamed. Faint teardrops wetted the corners of his eyes. "I do know the way to the queen."

"You're willing to take sides that there's only one? Not three or twenty or one hundred?"

The boy smiled and let out a soft laugh. "Just one. Though she has the kind of magic that would make her seem a thousand."

"That's good because I need to find my father, and if she's as powerful as that, then she should be able to help."

The boy's eyes looked downcast again.

"What is it?" asked Gwen.

"You'll have a terrible time getting her to help

you. You're human." He said the word like it was the name of the devil.

"Well," began Gwen, "does that really matter? I've got magic inside of me, you know."

The boy's eyes widened. "Do you?"

"Yes. Though I can't quite remember how it came to be." Gwen searched her memory. She knew that she had been given a spell to swallow, but she couldn't remember how or who had given it to her. All she could see when she recalled it was a vision of the twilight sky and stars swirling in the darkness.

"'Tis good you have a spell," said the boy. "That's right good." The way he looked at her then was strange, as if searching for something or trying to recall the details of a memory. The look passed quickly and the boy nodded. "Maybe the queen will listen at least."

"Then we can be partners?" asked Gwen.

"If you'll have me."

Gwen smiled, but the corners of her mouth turned down. "How is it you know the way to the queen when all those others did not?"

A blush rose to the boy's cheeks. "I- I don't exactly know the way myself..." he stammered. "But I know the one who does," he added quickly.

"If we are to be partners," said Gwen, "first we must tell each other the truth. Can you do that?"

"Aye," said the boy, "The truth is I used to prentice with a wood grue named Thorn, and he serves the queen. Brings her treasures from the forest, and it was when I served him that I saw her, and he can tell us the way to her abode, I'm sure of it." He said this speech quickly, the words slipping off his tongue like ice.

"And you're willing to help me find this wood grue?"

"Aye! If we can find the queen then she just might..."

"Might what? I thought we were telling the truth."

The boy blushed again. "You're right. The truth is I hope she can lift my curse. Maybe if I take you to her, we can both get something for our troubles."

Gwen was satisfied. "That's good. And after the truth," she continued, "we must tell each other our names."

"Alright. My name is Tom."

Gwen laughed. "Tom? Do all the pucks in this forest take such human names?"

"It's not a human name!" he said, scowling. "I thought we were supposed to be trusting each other."

Gwen nodded. "You're right. That was a bad jest. I'm sorry, Tom. My name is Gwenhivar."

Tom nodded his head, but Gwen could see his face was still stormy. "Your name's as strange as mine," he said, sulking.

"It's not strange where I come from," she replied, then bit her lip. Truthfully, her name was unusual. "My father is a lord, and mine is a good name for a lord's daughter."

"The queen'll want to know if your father is a lord."

"Will she really?"

"Aye, she goes for that sort of thing. Some say she once had a prince for a husband, but he died, so now she weeps for him and tries to find something to fill her heart."

"Is that what all the faerie knights are for?"

Tom shrugged. "I don't know. But the queen will like to know you come from such lineage."

"I hope she will." Gwen thought for a moment. *What sort of person was this queen?* she wondered. Somehow in her mind, she thought the queen would be solemn and mysterious, not someone who pined for a lost lover and made husbands out of tree branches. Would this heartbreak make the queen more compassionate or more cruel? Either way, Gwen knew she had no other choice. She was an outsider in this forest, and lost, and utterly unsure of what to do. The queen would have to be her only hope if she wanted to find her father. And Tom. He was her hope too if he could help her find the queen.

"Shall we shake hands and be off?" She didn't know if the creatures in this wood shook hands, but it was all she could think to do.

Tom held out an unenthused palm, and Gwenhivar took it. When she began to shake it firmly and amiably, Tom's scowl faded and his cheeks brightened a little.

"Partners," Gwen said.

"Partners," echoed Tom.

"Now to your friend Thorn."

"Aye, my friend." For a brief moment, Tom looked back as if worried something was following them. But they were alone and the wind began to blow.

The forest darkened as they traveled, and the trees swayed with every gust of the wind.

"A storm?" asked Gwen, but Tom shook his head.

"Winds come and go, and skies darken and don't, but often there are no storms. It's just the way of things here."

"Everything is so strange." Gwen shivered. "I'm still not used to it."

"How did you come by this woods?"

"My father. I fell over the edge into the forest, and he rushed in to rescue me. That's when..." She hesitated. She worried suddenly that the fairies were listening.

"When what?" asked Tom. His round eyes stared at her. They had both stopped walking, and the wind swirled around them.

"They took him," Gwen finished. She had whispered the words.

Tom's eyes widened. He understood, and a shadow passed over his face.

"That's why I must find him," said Gwen, her voice stronger now. She knew she couldn't lose heart, even though the strange coldness was creeping through her again. It wasn't a cold from without, but within.

"It won't be easy," replied Tom, "not if you think *they've* got him."

"But the queen?" Gwen's voice grew anxious.

"I dunno." Tom didn't elaborate. Instead, he started walking again.

On and on they went, and for Gwen, it seemed like hours. The wind blew so bitterly that her cheeks began to sting, and her eyes watered. Tom seemed less bothered by the biting gale. He marched in front of her, resolute. But soon the wind grew even stronger, swirling around them like a cyclone, bending trees like they were dandelion stems, and pushing the children back the way they had come. Gwen lifted her arm to shield her face, and with her head down, she tried to force her way through. Tom, for his part, stayed in front of her and took the brunt of the wind's strength. But the gusts were so powerful that both Tom and Gwen could feel their feet lifting off the ground at times, their clothes and limbs caught by the wind like sails billowing above the sea.

"Tom!" cried Gwen. "We can't go on! We need shelter!"

Tom shook his head and furrowed his brow. "Nay! We're almost there!"

"But the wind! We'll be torn to shreds if we keep going!"

"It's up ahead! I can see Thorn's hut!" He pointed to the distance.

Her eyes stung when she tried to look ahead, the wind cutting across her face like a sharp axe. She could see nothing except more and more trees, all of them creaking and swaying in the storm.

But Tom kept up his slow march, and so Gwen followed. Whenever she took a step, however, the wind blasted itself upon her. It pushed her farther and farther away so that Tom was now well ahead. A gaping distance had formed between them, and Gwen worried she would lose sight of him in the thick trees.

The wind gushed again, and a hideous crack echoed through the woods. In an instant, a huge tree limb dropped to the forest floor. Gwen screamed, frozen with fear. The limb had fallen not even two feet in front of her, crashing to the ground and scattering debris in all directions. If she had only taken one more step, that limb would have crushed her.

Every part of her body shivered, as if tiny pins were pricking every inch of her skin. She could feel her heart pounding as if to burst. Tom was nowhere in sight, and the wind swirled. Trees started creaking and moaning, and Gwen thought she heard more splintering and cracking of wood.

The wind was trying to bring the forest down upon her. Wild frenzy overtook her, and she searched frantically for a place to hide, for some kind of shelter. But all about her was nothing but trees and the furious wind.

Another tree fell, slamming into the ground behind her. It was partially hollow, and as it struck the forest floor, shards of bark splintered and flew in every direction.

Gwen knew she couldn't stay here. Desperately, she turned to go back the way she and Tom had come. Perhaps if she gave up seeking the wood grue this storm would abate. Running blindly, she headed back in the direction where the faerie knight had died, but she hadn't gone far when someone grabbed her arm and swung her around.

"Where are you going!" cried Tom. "You can't go back!"

"Look!" Gwen screamed, pointing at the fallen trees. "They're trying to kill me!"

The wind hurled another tree limb from the sky, and Tom pulled Gwen out of the way just before it crashed down upon them. Having escaped death, Tom now understood. He nodded, and keeping his hand firmly entwined with Gwen's, he began to run, leading her away from the falling trees.

They had not gone more than a hundred yards when the windstorm suddenly stopped. Everything was as calm as an early dawn.

Noticing that his fingers still mingled with Gwen's,

Tom blushed and dropped her hand like a hot coal. Then he looked around, and neither he nor Gwen could believe they were standing in the same forest as the one that had just been ravaged by a deadly gale. The sun even began to peek out from behind the clouds.

"I think that was a warning," said Gwen, catching her breath.

Tom stared about, unsettled.

"Could something want to prevent us from finding the wood grue?" continued Gwen.

"I- I don't see why..." stammered Tom.

"The queen?"

Tom frowned then shook his head. "But why should she? She—" He stopped himself.

Gwen wondered what he had been about to say, but before she could ask, Tom spoke again.

"I have an idea," he said quickly. "A better way to find the queen."

"Perhaps I don't want to find her now."

"O' course you do! She's the only one I know who can help you find your father."

"But something is trying to stop me from finding her. What else could have caused the wind to target me so?"

Tom looked at her. His face said the words that neither one of them had wanted to say earlier. *The fairies. The ones who had taken Gwen's father.*

"What is this better way?" asked Gwen.

"It's farther," answered Tom. "That's why I didn't mention it earlier. But it'll show us the way to the queen better than Thorn. He can sometimes be sour, and hard to bargain with. But the pool don't ask for anything, only our gaze."

"The pool?"

"Aye, they say it's made of glass, but when one looks upon it and asks a question, it'll show the answer."

Gwen's eyes gleamed. "Why, that's brilliant! I won't even need to find the queen, I'll just ask the pool to show me my father!"

This didn't seem to suit Tom at all. He started stammering and muttering that the queen would still need to be consulted, that the glass pool might not show her things so plainly, that it would be good to ask the queen for help because such journeys as these were hard and full of several dangers.

"Nothing's more powerful than the queen, and if your father's being held prisoner—" he broke off and didn't dare utter the name of the fairies. "Well then, we'll need her help, that's all."

"If you say so," replied Gwen. "I'm not opposed to finding the queen. I just thought that we could do things on our own."

Tom shook his head. "That gets you into trouble in these woods."

"Is that why you're helping me? So neither of us is on our own?" Gwen meant it kindly, but Tom looked away and couldn't meet her face.

"We'd best be off," he said, at last, staring into the distance. "Long journey to the pool."

The trees around them were as calm as ever, but Gwen felt a coldness run through her veins. "Tom," she said in a low voice, "what's to stop the wind... or *something else*... from preventing us again?"

Tom understood and looked around and behind, just as he'd done before when they'd first set off.

"It's a risk," he agreed, satisfied that nothing was nearby. "But what else can you do?"

"I could leave these woods and forget my father," Gwen said coolly.

Tom's eyes widened. "But—"

"I won't do that. I can't." Fire was back in the girl's face, and she looked eagerly at Tom. "The wind will have to break me first."

Tom gave her a strange look as if her skin had turned to stone, but then he shrugged and started walking.

He led her to a rivulet that cut through the forest. "We should follow this for several miles," he said. "It empties into a glade, and there they say is the glass pool."

"They say? Have you never been to it?"

"Nay, but I know it's there. I've heard many true tales."

Gwen felt a twinge of doubt at Tom's words, but she had little choice. She had to hope.

They walked on, following the path of the rivulet. Dragonflies and water striders danced above the water, and Gwen thought she saw tiny golden fish splash and glide across the rocky bottom. At times, even the water itself seemed to coalesce into shapes and figures that moved through the current. These shapes reminded Gwen of little crabs and mollusks, but every once in a while they shifted and grew into faces made of rocky sand, leering up at her from the streambed bottom.

She looked at Tom to see if he noticed anything, but he was oblivious. As she watched him, she tried to see any hint of the puckish creature he claimed to be. While those other pucks had long noses or fat noses, moss and lichen growing on their skin, and eyes the color of amber, Tom looked as ordinary as any human boy. She wondered what or who had cursed him but couldn't find the courage to ask. Upsetting him might mean losing his help.

After more than an hour, the rivulet started to widen into a larger stream, and the water turned murky and muddy brown. Out of the corner of her eye, Gwen still thought she saw faces forming in the current: hideous faces with crooked smiles. But every time she tried to scrutinize the faces, they disappeared, turning into ordinary river water. She looked at Tom again, but his eyes were fixed on the distance up ahead, searching through the trees.

"Stream'll split soon," he said. "We must follow the western way."

"And find the glass pool?"

Tom nodded.

"What if we took the other way?"

"North? Nay, I wouldn't advise it. Fire toads and mud gnomes and worse things still. The forest turns sickly up there. Besides, the pool is to the west."

"How big is this forest?"

"Bigger than I can say. Some claim it's as big as the world."

Gwen laughed. "That's silly. I know for a fact that it's not."

"Do you?" Tom raised a mocking eyebrow.

"Of course! I came from outside the forest, remember? I fell over the edge. Something can't have an edge if it's the whole world. There is much more to the world than this forest."

"You seem sure of yourself."

"I just know, that's all."

Tom shook his head. "I've never seen any edge of the forest."

"Perhaps I'll show you." Gwen stuck her tongue out. Then she tagged him and began to run, scurrying along the bank. "Catch me if you can!"

Tom beamed. "You can't outrun a puck, you know!" he cried.

He hurried after her, and the two of them danced along the edge of the stream, their feet skipping over the leaves and rocks. They ran a furious race, and although she started first, Gwen found herself slipping behind Tom. He was too lithe and quick, his toes nimble enough to evade every stone or tree root that threatened to trip him. His speed was impossible, and Gwen realized that she was no match. Her feet started aching; a stitch in her side made her wince. Puffing great gasps of air, she finally surrendered. Tom was well ahead of her, a small figure in the distance. Jogging a bit to catch up, Gwen called out.

"You win, Tom! I give up!" She laughed despite herself. It felt good to run barefoot through the woods, and the little golden fish in the stream splashed their tails as they swam alongside her. Her feet were darkened with soil and dirt; the skirt of her dress was as murky as dirty dishwater. But Gwenhivar didn't care. She felt a pulsing energy throb through her chest, even as she tried to catch her breath and head toward Tom.

But when she looked, she saw nothing. Tom was gone.

Gwen looked to the west; she looked across the stream; she searched everywhere. She started to run again, to reach the place where Tom had been, but there was no sign of him. She cried out for him. She groped through the trees, keeping the stream in sight, looking everywhere.

At last, she returned to the water and gazed into the stream. It was as glorious as ever, with dragonflies the color of amber flitting in all directions, and the water sparkling in the sun. The golden fish, however, were gone.

The creeping fear which was always lurking just beneath her skin began to surface. It crawled along her flesh and then it sank into her stomach. It carved a hole inside of her.

She was alone. Tom had disappeared. One thought kept sliding through her head: *They have taken him. Just like…*

That's when Gwenhivar noticed the heavy sound of falling water. Nearby, the stream was emptying into a deep pool.

She followed the water's course as the ground sloped downward. The trees were tall and thick here. It was an old part of the forest, and the canopy of leaves blocked out most of the sun. The stream emptied into a shaded valley, and as Gwen peered down, she saw it: a pool of shining silver water. Inexplicably, the water in the pool did not move, even as the stream emptied into it. No ripple, no wave. Only stillness.

Like a mirror of perfect glass.

CHAPTER FOUR

THE GLASS POOL OF THE HIDDEN WEST

"A feast," said the red voice.

"Aye, no faerie knight this," said the dark voice. "Real blood."

"He's been picked over," said the last voice. "But still worthy."

They crept towards Agravaine, slithering out of the thicket and into the open air. Agravaine groaned and lolled his head in a stupor against the tree. He was covered in small nicks and scratches, but the wounds had begun to scab. The three hungered for him.

But no sooner had they emerged, did the old ones retreat. Softer footfalls padded toward them. They did not tarry. Without another sound, they fled.

A gentle hand brushed against Agravaine's face and touched a lock of his hair. Breath—warm and sweet—filled his nostrils. A laugh like water falling over rocks awakened him, and his eyes beheld a woman. She knelt beside him and smiled.

"Don't fear," she said. "Your troubles are at an end."

Then she turned her head and spoke to someone unseen. "He will do quite nicely. Take him."

Agravaine felt his body being lifted, felt himself becoming weightless. He was at the mercy of this unseen force, and being too weak to even speak, he let it carry him away.

The woman's quiet footsteps followed close behind, beating a soft lullaby in Agravaine's ear until he fell into a swoon and slept a dreamless sleep.

ॐ

Gwenhivar knew she could ask the glass pool only one question. She had come this far to ask for the queen, for her father, for some way to find them both. But now the question that rose to her lips was for Tom.

Where could he be?

She wanted to say it aloud, but her veins filled with ice when she thought of it. Once again, a strange feeling of coldness crept into her chest. She knew what she wanted to say, but she felt no desire to say it. Her father was the one she needed to find, not Tom. Hovering over the mirror-like water, she searched her own face for answers.

Is that me? she wondered.

Her eyes looked sunken, and her skin ashen. She looked like she hadn't slept in weeks. But what disturbed her most of all was her hair. It was still the color of golden wheat, but there was a kind of lessening in its brightness. The wheat had been stricken with some blight that made it dull and tinged with pale ivory. She shivered at her reflection and remembered what had happened to her dress.

Looking down, she saw once again that the skirt was colorless; the bright sapphire was gone.

Gwen knew something about herself was changing, but she couldn't explain or articulate what it was. A growing feeling, an intuition, that was all. But she knew it was happening. When she gazed once again at the pool, it felt as if she was looking through a window at a stranger.

I must ask for Tom, she thought again. She hardly knew him, and yet she could not abandon him. Perhaps together they could find another way to her father.

"Is that what you think?" The voice who spoke was behind her.

No. It was next to her. No, it was several voices.

Gwen searched in every direction. Nothing.

"You can't find him that way," the voices continued. "Won't work."

Something about these voices taunted Gwen; they seemed to sneer at her when they spoke. Defiant, Gwenhivar leaned over the placid water and asked her question. "Where is Tom, the cursed puck?"

She waited, but as the seconds ticked by and nothing happened, she asked again, louder and more insistent.

"Where is Tom, the cursed puck? The boy who led me here and disappeared? Tell me where I can find him!"

Nothing.

"We told you it wouldn't work." The voices jeered at her. "Can't find him that way."

Then Gwen noticed the worms. They crawled atop the dark soil beneath her hands and feet as she knelt by the pool. Small as inch worms and colored a deep, bloody red, the worms gathered by the dozens. When they spoke, it was one voice and many.

"We'll tell you the secret," they said.

Gwen felt the hairs on her arms and neck quiver; the worms were crawling over her fingers now. She wanted to stand up and fling them away, but she tried to stay still.

"What is the secret?" she whispered.

The worms began to crawl up her arms, leaving streaks of red ochre on her skin. "Only we can see the answers. Only we."

Now the revulsion was too strong. Gwen leaped up and tried to knock the worms off her arms, but they stuck to her like leeches. Quickly, they slithered up her arms, onto her shoulders, then up her neck, and onto her face.

"No!" Gwen cried, but it was too late. The worms crawled into her eyes, boring into the corners of the eye sockets, blinding her.

She saw nothing.

Then she saw the glass pool, hovering before her like a mirror upon a wall.

Tell me where I can find him. The voices came from within her head, the unified voices of the bloodworms. But as they spoke inside her, the mirror listened. The silvery glass shimmered and melted away, and a world came into view.

It was a world of mud and clay, and like a primordial ooze, the mud roiled and churned until it began to bubble up, expanding upward and coalescing into a small, stout body. The mud became flesh, and a stern cruel face stared out through the vision. He wore a charred pinewood crown upon his head. Sitting at his turbid feet was a boy, sandy-haired and pale, with the cursed face of a human. The boy's hands and feet were encased in hardened clay, and the mud king laughed. His murky face was bulbous and malformed, both alien and familiar.

This is the king of the mud gnomes.

And Tom was his prisoner.

Gwen searched the vision for some weakness in the mud king, for anything that could break those clay shackles around Tom, but just as mud washes away in clean water, the image melted into a crystal sheen. Gwen tried to close her eyes—to break the vision—but her eyes were not her own. The bloodworms owned them.

What they saw next was the face of a man.

Father!

Gwen's stomach churned as violently as the oozing mud from earlier. Lord Agravaine's face was pale, his eyes closed. He was being carried by something which Gwen could not see, but his body bounced along gently, and every once in a while, a slender hand came into view and brushed the hair from his face or caressed his cheek.

Gwen feared her father was dead, but her fear was overpowered by the sight of that willowy hand. She wanted to see more, to discover to whom that hand belonged. She tried to will the vision to show her, to move its gaze so that she could see the figure who walked beside her father, but instead, she saw what they were walking towards.

The forest opened up into a clearing, and standing in the center was a pair of wrought-iron gates. They were not part of any larger wall or fence, and they did not guard anything in particular. They stood alone in the clearing as if abandoned. But as the retinue which bore her father proceeded, the gates suddenly swung open, and Lord Agravaine and his companions passed through, the vision suddenly shimmered and changed.

She saw her father laughing. He smiled with delight, his hands outstretched, clasping someone else's slender, gentle hands. Together entwined, they were caught up in a spinning, reckless dance. Agravaine looked much younger. He spun and whirled, hand in hand with someone unseen, until the hands let go, a raven cried death into the sky, and tears washed away everything.

Gwen squeezed her eyes shut as hard as she could. She felt the worms spasm and wriggle, but she squeezed all the harder, until at last, their fleshy bodies burst and blood spilled from the corners of her eyes. When she opened them, the last drops of blood leaked out, and then they were dry.

The forest glade was silent.

Gwen wasn't sure why that last vision had made her weep, but now her eyes stung from dryness as if she had shed so many tears that none were left.

Did I really cry that much?

Gwen couldn't remember. But when she looked again at the glass pool, she saw her reflection, and in her eyes, she saw a new and terrible dullness. No longer were they bright blue. Instead, like tepid water in a tide pool, her eyes were gray, and her cheeks were stained with blood.

"How odd," she murmured, but she didn't seem to care. Her father might not recognize her when she found him, but this thought didn't trouble her. In fact, she felt quite calm when she thought of her father. He seemed untroubled in the vision; asleep, perhaps, but unhurt. Any fear she had about his death was gone. Curiosity, instead, overwhelmed her.

Who had been that woman he was dancing with? Was she the same as the one who accompanied him through the iron gates? Where did those gates lead?

All these questions and more circled through her head, but the vision had been little help in showing her the way to find her father.

"But Tom," she said to herself. She did know the way to Tom. The cruel king, with his bulbous face and body of wet clay, was a mud gnome. And didn't Tom say the stream turned north to that realm? To fire toads and mud gnomes and worse things still?

Gwenhivar wished she had some form of protection, and perhaps even some weapon to help set Tom free.

Then, as if in answer to her wish, the glass pool cracked.

The deep fissure that ran down the middle of the pool revealed something metallic beneath. Gwen leaned over and reached her hand between the jagged edges of the crack. She could see now that the pool was indeed not made of water or even ice but of some other substance, something almost glass-like but different. It was like foam that had been frozen and polished to a sheen. Beneath the surface, she saw hard rock, black as obsidian, covering the bottom of the pool. But this rocky surface was not what glinted beneath. Her hand felt the cold metal, the links looped together one by one, the heaviness of it, and the length. Gwen pulled it forth from the pit.

An iron chain.

It was several feet long, and the links were sturdy. Gwen turned it over in her hands, puzzled. She didn't see how this would help. It was cumbersome, and she had no good way to carry it, but Gwen felt it would be wrong to leave the chain behind. The pool had given it to her, after all. She wrapped it around her waist a few times, then slung the remaining length over her shoulder. Restricted by the iron links which now bound her, she had to move more slowly.

And yet, as she began to walk back along the edge of the stream, she felt a strange comfort. The chain was like her armor.

Without a glance back, Gwen left the silent grove and headed towards the fork in the stream and the way north.

CHAPTER FIVE

THE HIGH CLIFFS OF THE MUD LORD

The voice which spoke to Tom in the dark was deep and heavy. It tried to feign kindness, but insincerity dripped from it like sludge.

"I do not desire sacrifice," the voice said. "But I cannot build my empire alone. If I'm to rule the north and push my way to the edges of Illvelion, I'll need an empire. You, my servant, shall help me build it. Think what glory awaits you as you aid in my destiny! Think what ecstasies! I am giving you a great gift. You shall be like the footstool of an emperor. No need to thank me now. When all our efforts are complete, then you may kiss my feet."

Tom knew he was in a dark crevice, trapped in the side of the mud cliffs. He'd been a prisoner for only a short while, but it felt like forever. He couldn't move his arms or his legs, and the tight quarters made it difficult to breathe. When the cold, wet hands of the mud gnomes grabbed him and pulled him into the daylight, he was blinded at first and shocked by the warmth of the summer sun. He sucked in a gulp of fresh air.

When his eyes adjusted, he saw the king of the mud gnomes standing over him. No taller than Tom, the Mud Lord made up for his short stature with his girth. He was as wide as he was tall, and every inch of him was made of thick, solid earth, packed tightly into a body of hardened clay. A crown of charred pinewood sat upon his square head.

"You are paler than I remember," the Mud Lord said. "You'll burn in the sun, and we can't have that." Reaching down, he scooped up a handful of clay and began to smear it all over Tom's arms and legs and across his face. "Better. Much better."

With a fat finger, the king commanded his soldiers to carry Tom away. As they grabbed him and hurried him along to his enslavement, Tom caught sight of where he was. High atop a ridge, he saw the forest below spread itself over the world like a sea of pine and aspen.

"To the mines!" cried the gnome king. It was the last thing Tom heard before he descended.

❧

"We know her," said the red voice. "But she's grown smaller."

"Almost the same as we," said the dark voice.

"Nay," said the last voice, "she is not. She is a puck, cursed by the grue. Like the other one."

Gwenhivar was asleep, but she heard the voices. A blanket of thick mud had grown over her, and the sun had baked it into clay. She lay quietly, lost in dreams of her father. The voices came into her dreams softly, like gentle breezes.

The old ones crept closer, their fingers curling into the strands of her hair.

"Dull," whispered the red voice.

"Aye," said the dark voice.

"Careful," hissed the last voice.

Gwenhivar stirred, but the blanket of hard clay held fast. When her body realized its prison, she began to struggle, her eyes squeezed shut. Her slumber was not an ordinary one, for as she struggled, she seemed to fall deeper into her dreams. What she saw in them, the old ones couldn't tell, but her face was grim and her struggles violent. Still, the clay did not crack.

"Shall we fly?" asked the red voice.

"Nay," said the dark voice.

"Watch," said the last voice.

Gwen's struggle abated; her body had given up. But her lips mumbled words now as she dreamed.

"Father?" wondered the red voice.

"Something lost," answered the dark voice.

"Listen," said the last voice. "She calls."

Indeed, Gwen was calling out now in her sleep, first for her father, but then for something else. The three listened and wondered at the words she spoke.

"Shall we?" asked the red voice.

"She does not name us," said the dark voice.

"True," said the last voice. "But still."

The other two looked at the last. He moved silently towards the girl. Then, with a fingernail sharp as a thorn, he pricked the skin of her cheek. The tiniest drop of blood swelled there, and Gwen cried out.

Her eyes opened, and she saw the face of the last fairy. She would not have named it *fairy*, for though it was small, there was little about it that resembled the pictures in her nursery books. Scales covered its thin body and fur its narrow head, and it had a long tail like a rat. Its eyes were huge and bulbous—frog-like —and dark as ink, protruding from the top of its head like swelling bubbles. Long fingers hung from its twig-like arms: three fingers each with three sharp fingernails.

Gwen knew she should be frightened, but she was not. Here was a creature unlike any she had ever seen, even more strange than the twisted animals she had watched devour the faerie knight, and yet she was unperturbed by it. It seemed as unremarkable as a fox or a fish.

"You called out," said the last fairy.

"We answered," said the red.

Gwen saw this fairy now too. It slinked closer and looked nothing like the one which had pricked her, but somehow Gwen knew the two were kin. The red fairy resembled a leathery bat, rose-red and utterly sightless, for it had no eyes above its snout-like nose. It sensed Gwen despite its seeming blindness and groped toward her, pulling itself forward by the sharp claws at the end of each wing.

Last of all crept the dark one. A shadow. A shapeless thing. It was a cloud and a fog and a wisp of black smoke. Gwen couldn't say what it was, but she knew it was as much a creature as the other two, and when it spoke, a face and mouth appeared, teeth as sharp as wind.

"The bargain shall be struck," it said, the dark voice resounding like a cavern's echo.

Gwen felt a curious thrill at such a word, but why she would feel excitement in striking a bargain with such creatures, she did not know. Her utter lack of fear or apprehension was disconcerting, and she could hardly believe the calmness in her voice when she asked, "Are you saying you can get me out?"

"We can," said the red fairy.

"For a price," whispered the dark fairy.

"For a partnership," the red fairy corrected.

"You called out," said the last fairy, the one with scales and fur.

"I did?" said Gwen, searching her memory.

"In your sleep," replied the fairy, its rat tail swishing back and forth.

The drop of blood on Gwen's cheek began to roll down. With his long, thorny fingernail, the fairy lifted it from her skin and held it before her like a droplet of red dew.

"Here is the bargain price," said the fairy.

"What am I giving you with that?" Gwen was clever enough to know that blood was dangerous to bargain with.

All three fairies smiled toothsome grins, but the dark fairy answered. "The partnership, of course."

Gwen wanted to press the matter, to see what this partnership entailed, but the three fairies didn't give her a chance. The dark fairy scooped up a handful of mud, while the red fairy spat into it, and together the two fashioned a small bowl out of the clay.

Then, taking the bowl from the other two, the last fairy placed the drop of blood inside, and with quick hands, he formed a ball, enclosing the blood within the clay. Within a few moments, the clay was hardened into a stone. The fairy tossed it into the air and cackled delightedly when he caught it.

"Now," he said. With the lightest touch, he tapped

the ball of hardened clay against Gwen's enclosure. From the point of contact, thousands of thin cracks appeared in the clay blanket, rippling across the surface. Then, like shattered glass, the stone broke apart into piles of tiny pieces. Gwen was free.

But the three fairies were not ready for what they saw. When her bonds were destroyed, Gwen was released, but she was still wrapped in the iron chain. It encircled her waist, and the loose end hung over her shoulder.

When the fairies saw this, they screeched like terrified rodents caught in a cat's paws. Quicker than wind, they scurried, flying down the hill and into the depths of the forest.

It all happened so fast, Gwen wasn't sure what to make of it. She lifted the chain from her shoulder and examined it; it was as ordinary as ever. Perhaps its power was to keep such enemies as those fairies away, in which case, she was glad to be wrapped in it.

But what of the bargain? The fairy with scales and fur still had her blood in the clay stone. Gwen decided to ignore her unease and focus on the task at hand. She was free and close to the realm of the mud gnomes. The stream here had diminished into a smaller rivulet, and looming above her was the silver-gray cliffside covered in wet clay. She left the waters behind and began to climb.

The weight of the chain made her trek more difficult. The heavy iron weighed her down even more now than it had earlier, and she felt as if gravity itself was trying to crush her. She thought of herself as an ant carrying five times its weight. There was a curious paradox between the external weight of the chain and the almost hollow feeling which she felt growing inside. This feeling was more than the coldness from before; it was a sense that her insides were being cleared out for something new, like a farmer removing stones from the untilled ground. The heaviness of the chain was in strong contrast to this inner emptiness.

But heavy though it was, the chain still comforted her. She held to it tightly. The thought that it was a kind of armor returned. It had warded off the three fairies, perhaps it would do the same for the mud gnomes.

The ground flattened out and Gwen found herself standing on a plateau. There was a higher cliff still above, but this plateau stretched a long way to the east and even sloped down a little at the horizon. The mud here was dried up as if baked by the sun. The earth was covered with cracks and fissures, and mounds of hardened clay dotted the area.

In the distance, Gwen thought the mounds seemed to take on more distinct shapes, like sculptures. As she approached them, she was sure they were meant to be crafted figures, though they were crude and ill-formed. To her mind, they looked like chess pieces that had been covered by mud and allowed to harden. Some were taller than her and some were quite small, no bigger than a badger. They all were in strange poses, some with arms outstretched, some hunched over and reaching toward the ground.

One, in particular, caught Gwen's attention for the clay that formed it still gleamed a bit with moisture, as if it hadn't started to harden until just recently. She came closer, noticing that the shape was human-like and similar to her own. A child, perhaps.

When she came quite close, the clay began to quiver and pieces of it flaked off. A tiny earthquake rumbled within. Gwen feared the whole thing would crumble into dust, so she backed away, and as soon as she was several paces removed, the quivering stopped and the statue stilled.

The whole place took on a sinister quality now, and the statues seemed almost alive. She decided to pass by quickly and make for higher slopes, but just then a sharp breeze blew and flakey dust blew off the statue she had disturbed. An infinitesimal speck of color blazed through the gray mud.

Strands of hair, the color of sand.

"Tom!" Gwen's heart leaped and almost seemed to hurt. She hurried toward the statue—which wasn't a statue after all—and when she was almost upon it, it began to quiver again and clumps of powdery clay broke off and crumbled to the ground. Gwen had no idea why her presence should make the clay crumble, but soon Tom's head and shoulders, then his chest and arms, then finally his legs and feet were free and he fell into the rubble. A light coating of mud covered his clothes and skin.

Was this the power the fairies had given her? But if so, then what power was it and how did it work? Gwen felt nothing in particular when the clay had been breaking, no power welling inside or coursing through her. Just that hollowness she had felt before.

"Tom!" Gwen called again, but his eyes were closed and he looked fast asleep. She bent over and did her best to pull him out of the rubble. But even once she had him free, he did not stir. Gentle shaking did nothing and calling his name even less than nothing. He looked like one dead, but Gwen could see the shallow ups and downs of his chest as he breathed. She wished suddenly that the three fairies would appear again and do something. It was a wild thought—for the fairies terrified her—but she could think of nothing else to do. The chain had made them flee. What if she took it off? Would they return?

Quickly, Gwen lifted the chain from her shoulders and unwound it from her waist. She found one of the larger statues and hid the chain as best she could behind it. As she did so, she wondered why these other statues were as still as solid rock. No crumbling, no breaking free for the inhabitants inside. She felt her flesh prickle as she realized the captives within were most likely dead.

When she had hidden the chain and stood up, she knew something had changed. Her whole body felt different. It was lighter, to be sure, but it wasn't the lightness she noticed. It was the power. She realized now that the chain had been holding something back, or perhaps keeping something at bay. The emptiness she had felt earlier was gone, replaced by an energy that vibrated through every vein.

Looking at the statues again, she realized that if she wanted to, she could crush their hard clay into powder or swell them with water again and turn the stone into mud. She could even take the raw clay from the ground and fashion her own statue if she wished. This is what the fairies had given her. And the chain had been suppressing this power. She smiled and thought how glad she was to be rid of such shackles. How could she have ever found comfort in that chain?

When she pressed her hand against one of the nearby stone statues, she felt the flakes of hardened mud shudder. Within a few seconds, the whole thing had crumbled to dust. There was nothing inside, or else whatever had been inside was long ago reduced to nothingness. Gwen looked around at the other statues and wondered if she should do the same to all of them. Perhaps then she could make her own monuments.

Reaching down, she scooped up a bit of wet clay. She expected it to be cold, but it was quite warm in her hands. Unconsciously, she began to mold the clay. After a minute or two, she looked down and saw a figure of a man, exquisitely detailed and lifelike. Gwen should have been shocked by the skill of the little clay figure, but instead, she regarded it dispassionately.

It looked like someone she knew, but she couldn't quite recognize the face. Suddenly dissatisfied, she crushed it and threw it back onto the ground. It was then that Tom woke up.

"Hullo," he mumbled. "Didn't expect you here."

But Gwen wasn't listening. She was climbing up the next cliff, driven by an insatiable desire to see past the plateau and out into the east. Tom followed her as best he could, but he was still weak from his ordeal, and Gwen seemed driven by some mad desire.

When she reached the top of the next cliff, she saw what was on the other side. The flatness of the plateau transformed into rolling hills of thick, dark mud. Atop these hills stood the unfinished metropolis of the Mud Lord. Towers and minarets and palaces filled the skyline, but all of them were misshapen and covered with grotesqueries that made Gwen recoil. Hideous visages and nightmarish shapes spilled over the sides of the buildings and cascaded down like vomitous sewage, and the mud and muck from the ground below roiled up like a sea of tar, spilling over the slaves who worked to construct the city.

The slaves were all sorts—imps, grues, nixies, pucks—and they shoveled and shaped the mud as best they could, but the mud had a mind of its own, covering their faces, dripping into their eyes, choking them as huge globs gushed from below like geysers. The slaves looked like slugs, covered in their mucky slime, struggling to regain their footing and continue their hideous servitude.

Gwen felt anger swelling in her heart. She knew nothing of these creatures other than they suffered, and she felt the power inside herself begin to grow.

"Blimey," whispered Tom, for he had now reached the peak of the cliff too. "That's where I'd be if I hadn't been baked into a statue."

"It's cruel," said Gwen, keeping her eyes fixed on the Mud Lord's kingdom.

"True enough," replied Tom. "Many things are cruel. That's the way of the world."

"For shame, Tom," said Gwen, her eyes narrowing in fury. "We cannot let such things go unchallenged."

Tom didn't understand what she meant. Wasn't it enough that he was free, that they could fly from this hideous kingdom, that they could continue their journey to find the queen?

But Gwen seemed possessed of another idea, an urge that Tom did not understand nor foresee. She closed her eyes and her face tightened. Then the ground beneath them began to shake. The earth undulated like waves rolling to the shore, and all the towers and minarets of the Mud Lord's city rose and fell like flotsam floating atop the sea. The foundation of the earth was beginning to crack.

Seeing the city unmoored, the slaves were awakened from their drudgery. Shaking off their chains of slime, they started to clamber away from the pits and geysers, heading down the slopes of the cliff. They knew something worse was coming.

Gwen felt every muscle inside her body strain and tighten. She felt that the earth was at her command. If she wished it, she could make the whole hideous city fall in upon itself, or instead, she could raise it to new heights, refashioning the grotesqueries into marvels.

Somewhere in the distance, Tom was saying something, but she couldn't understand. She wasn't even thinking about the slaves now. All she thought was how wonderful it was to have such power. Balling her hands up into fists, she willed the city to destruction. Everything faltered. The earth split into a thousand fissures.

Then, like belching demons, huge creatures of obsidian and gravel rose from the mud. Red as hot coals, they burst through the thick mud, spraying muck in every direction. Croaking, their flaming tongues emerged like fiery whips and shot out to grab the fleeing prisoners. Imps and nixies and pucks screamed as they were devoured like flies.

No! Gwen tried to cry out, but her plea only rose as high as her heart. This was not what she had intended. This was not what she would command. More of those hideous fire toads erupted from the ground. The whole world seemed in ruin.

The earth shook again, unbidden, and Gwen lost

her footing. Mud bubbled into sludge from the heat of the toads, and soon the ground beneath her feet was falling away, sliding down the slopes.

Tom called for her as the mudslide took him down. He stretched a hand, but Gwen was too far. Then she too was slipping, down the waterfall of mud, toward the rocks and the stream far below.

As she fell, she watched the peaks of the vast city cave in upon themselves, and the flames of the fire toads streaked across the sky. Somewhere in the distance, a wrathful voice cried out.

Down, down below the suffocating mud she fell. Gwen couldn't breathe. Air was gone. All was clammy, cold, sticky mud. There was no more sunlight, no more sky. Only black and oily mud. And down she fell, or up, or sideways, or tumbled over. She couldn't tell any which way except for deeper: deeper into the sea of mud.

Then fingers found her wrist. Thin fingers and weak, but they wrapped themselves around her skin and held on tight until flecks of sun peppered the darkness, and then patches of blue and white, clouds and air, and Gwen could breathe again, and she swallowed air into her mouth like a desert nomad laps up cool water.

They were galloping. Tom held her tight, and together they rode a creature that could outrun the mudslide. Gwen still couldn't see clearly or find her bearings. All she knew was that she was out of the muck and mud, flying from the destruction, close to Tom.

They rode the air together back into the depths of the forest, carried by something—or someone—they did not know, and when exhaustion finally overtook them, they both fell into a deep and empty sleep.

The last thing they heard was the anguished curse of the Mud Lord echoing in the distance. It felt like a terrible and endless dream.

CHAPTER SIX

GALLIEN THE UNICORN

The stream burbled nearby, fast-moving over a bed of rocks. Gwen's eyes were open, but she had trouble focusing. She noticed she was still riding upon the creature. Tom sat in front of her, his head bowed in sleep. When she tried to look down, she got dizzy, for the height at which she sat was much greater than she expected. She had heard of such creatures as elephants—creatures in far-off lands—but she had never been able to imagine what it would be like to ride one.

Yet this creature was no elephant. It stood at least twelve feet tall at the shoulder, but its body was sleek and long, more like a gigantic red deer than a hulking pachyderm. As Gwen's eyes shook off their fog, they could see more clearly.

The skin of the creature was silver-white, and shimmering like stardust. It was a horse, but not a horse. It moved with equine grace but there was something about it that was almost serpentine, as if its body could grow longer or thinner at will. And its head was too massive even for a horse. When Gwen tried looking more closely at the head, it filled her vision. Its mane was like sea foam spreading out across the sand. Then rising from that foamy sea, a magnificent horn of gold pointed to the sky, and Gwen realized with a gasp what it was.

As if sensing her realization, the creature returned to a gallop, and its speed was so great and so sudden that Gwen swooned again and fell back into unconsciousness.

When she awoke again, she lay on the ground, the stars twinkling above her, and she and Tom were alone.

&

"Why does he still sleep?" the queen asked. Her tent was soaked with honeyed perfume, and the music which played from an unseen source was bright and full of the morning.

Outside, the night was clear and star-dappled, but inside the tent, it was as golden as summer. Smiling, the queen brushed a strand of hair from his forehead. His hair always seemed to fall across his brow and into his eyes. It stirred a memory in her, a giddiness that wiped away the long years of her life. But it was fleeting, and soon the hollowness within her breast returned. She wished a strand of his hair might fall again just so she could brush it away.

The queen knew his slumber was a spell, yet she had no antidote. *Once we pass through the gates,* she thought, *then he shall awaken.* But she wondered at this. For some time now, her magic seemed to have been weakening. Her faerie knights had fallen apart and decayed much faster these past few years. Wicked creatures from the north—mud gnomes and night wyrms—threatened the edges of her kingdom with their greed and hunger, and few of her spells repelled them. She slept fitfully every night because she feared hearing the whispers of the fairies at her windows. Perhaps even the gates would not be enough to break his curse.

She hummed softly with the music and studied the man's face. His dark hair was graying at the temples. Care and weariness etched themselves in the lines around his eyes and mouth. But he was not old. He was still flush with vitality, though his youthfulness was hidden behind the weight of responsibility. The queen understood. She too wore such a paradox.

But the source of it, she could not remember.

Gwen tried to concentrate on the stars. She wanted them to fill her vision and block out those other images: the swelling and cracking of the earth, the destruction of the Mud Lord's palace, the fire and clay, everything swallowed into darkness. Perhaps the stars would fill her up with their light and put an end to the ever-growing emptiness that settled in her chest. She didn't want to feel hollow and powerful at the same time; she wanted to be warm again.

But the stars emitted only cold light. They swam across her eyes like flecks of dust, and she remembered the way her dress had become faded and gray. Her hair too, and her eyes. Everything was draining out of her. She moved closer to Tom, hoping he could stem the tide.

He stirred. Soon he was wide awake and sitting up, searching the glade for something more than what he found. "Have you seen him?" he said to Gwen.

"Who?"

"Gallien."

The unicorn. Gwen did not say the words, but she remembered. She remembered the way it felt to be carried upon his back like she was riding the river itself.

"Is he friendly?" she asked.

Tom laughed at her ignorance. "Tis not the word for him. None that I know dare call him friend. But if he has carried us on his back, then I don't think we have much to fear."

Gwen didn't like the doubt which colored Tom's words. She felt her hollowness begin to swell. The power within grew. She could defend herself if need be. She would not let this creature hurt her if it came to that. She would bring forth such magic again that would shake the world...

But when she remembered the mane of sea foam and the golden horn, her dark thoughts dissipated and the hollowness felt smaller. She looked at Tom's face to find more warmth.

"Maybe he's gone," she said.

The sound of padding hooves put an end to that. Gallien the unicorn stood before them, emerging from the trees like a stream of moonlight passing through a cloud. He was larger than Gwen had remembered, a towering creature who made an ordinary equine look like a child's rocking horse. His horn burned forth from his forehead like a streak of lightning, and both children had to shield their eyes when he looked at them directly.

"Fortune favors you, children," he said, his voice much higher in pitch than Gwen expected, and it quivered like a horse's whinny. It was so unlike human speech, so airy and cold, that both children shivered and huddled close together. Gallien leaned his head in Gwen's direction and studied her. His eyes were dark and shimmered like the ocean under a full moon.

"A human child," he said. "A lord's daughter."

Gwen's skin prickled. She wondered how he knew her parentage.

"But there is something else..." Gallien's voice drifted off. "You have been making bargains."

"Tom and I are partners," Gwen answered defensively.

The unicorn shook his head, and the sea foam mane danced around him. "No," he said, "that is not what I meant. I speak of what you have given up."

Gwen swallowed her tongue. She remembered the draught from Troll-Hag and the way her dress was drained of its stardust. She remembered the drop of her blood, caught up in clay. And the three fairies, their voices dark and red.

"What do you mean, sir?" asked Tom. His voice swelled protectively. "Gwen's lost her father, but she didn't give him up. He was taken."

The unicorn snorted at Tom. "You defend her well, little puck. A fine guise you wear."

Tom shifted uncomfortably under Gallien's gaze. "I've been cursed," he muttered.

"Indeed. And now you seek to break the curse."

Tom didn't answer.

"Thank you for saving us," Gwen said, standing up. She felt it was time to leave. Something about Gallien's manner upset her; he seemed to be accusing them. "We owe you a debt of gratitude."

"And how will you repay your debt, then? Another bargain?" His dark eyes met hers; his horn blazed brightly.

Gwen looked away, reaching down to give Tom a hand up.

"We'll pay what you ask," she replied. "Within reason."

"You are in the forest now, human child. Reason holds no sway here."

Tom had said there was nothing to fear from Gallien, but Gwen was growing wary. The unicorn's words were far from amiable. He stood above them like a massive shadow, blocking out trees and stars from view, and Gwen decided she must summon some of her power lest he attack. She delved deep within and found the emptiness waiting for her. The ground beneath their feet was not so solid as it seemed; it might be moved if she could call upon it.

"What do you want?" she said, her voice rising with anger.

Gallien stamped the ground with his heavy cloven hoof, but when he shook his mane again, he seemed to lessen in size; the shadow passed. His horn still glowed, but his face was placid, and his gleaming coat was pearl-white. He looked like a shy pony, not the fearsome beast he had been moments before.

"I want to help you," he said gravely. "That is the price I ask."

Gwen didn't expect this. She tried to hold on to

the anger she had called forth, but it vanished like a stone dropping into the sea.

"We pay our debt by letting you help us?" Tom asked. "That seems topsy-turvy."

Gallien whinnied. "I told you reason holds no sway here. But do you accept my unreasonable demand?"

"If we do?" Gwen said, doing everything in her power to keep her guard up.

"Then I shall help you find the queen. After that, I cannot promise. What the queen decides and how she wills is not mine to judge, though I must have words with her. The Mud Lord has grown strong of late, and even though his mighty empire has been toppled, he will seek revenge and conquest. He is not content to let Illvelion be ruled by a queen once-human."

All of Gwen's guard was down now. "The queen is human?" She had not expected this. All she had known of the forest was that humans were unwanted; the fairies hunted them when they crossed the edge of the woods. Hadn't Troll-Hag told her she needed a spell to stay? Hadn't she been warned of the danger awaiting her father because of his humanity? Hadn't she herself faced such dangers? And now to find out that this land could be ruled by a human queen?

"Once-human," Gallien replied. "For she is no longer. Now she is..." He looked up into the stars and seemed lost in thought.

"Curse liked me," said Tom in answer to the silence. "Except reversed."

Gallien looked down at them again. "Something like that. Topsy-turvy, as you said."

A dark thought crossed Gwen's mind for a

moment, and she almost voiced it. *Am I cursed?* But she didn't want to know the answer. If she was cursed, she didn't want to break it. She found herself glad to be changing, to be something stronger than she once was. The girl who danced the fairy reel in the moonlit dew on the edge of the forest seemed a lifetime away. She had only played at freedom that night; now she felt it course through her veins. To be cursed was to be reborn. It didn't matter that her hair had lost its luster or that her eyes were graying; it didn't matter that she couldn't quite see the face of her father in her mind's eye anymore. She had something else now. Power. Magic.

Perhaps the queen felt the same, and that is why she ruled this land.

"Will you go with me?" Gallien asked, looking directly at Gwen. She was no longer the follower of Tom but the leader of their little pair.

"I will."

The unicorn nodded and then knelt before them. As his joints bent and his great body lowered itself to the ground, Gwen and Tom felt their breath catch in their throats. It was like watching a mountain kneel, or a wave land before them and turn into a pane of glass.

Gallien made himself low so that they might ascend upon his back. Gwen sat first, her fingers resting on the unicorn's thick neck; Tom sat behind her and held her waist.

As Gallien rose, the children felt themselves rising to the stars like firecrackers that would keep going and never burst. It was like being jettisoned to the mountain's peak.

When they looked across the glade and at the

stream, they felt like giants towering above the terrestrial sphere. The stars seemed closer, and for a moment, Gwen felt some regret that her dress had lost its sapphire glow. She wanted to shine as bright as these stars, to gleam in the darkness. But the feeling passed, and she forgot it.

Gallien set off. He galloped like rushing water, blurring the world around them. Gwen held on, and Tom to her, but never once did the children feel unsafe. They were part of the current, carried on by the wave.

As the moon set, the queen and her entourage approached the silent gates. Those around her shuddered before the cold iron, but the queen stood unafraid. It would pain her only a moment as she pressed upon the gates; it would be worse for her servants. When they passed through the gates, they would feel a burning in their skin that would not abate until she healed them with a spell. Her human prize would be safe from pain, but she hoped he might stir once they carried him through.

Of course, even if he didn't awaken, she could still keep him and watch him sleep and try to remember what had once filled the emptiness before she came to Illvelion. No more need for faerie knights made of acorns and stones, she hoped.

It was strange to hope this much, but the queen dared it. She was running out of time.

Stepping in front of the gates, she held out her long fingers and placed her palms on the wrought iron. It burned. An icy flame kissed her skin, searing the flesh. Tears filled her eyes—the same tears, always—but she would not abate. With great force, she moved the rusted hinges and flung wide the gates.

Her servants carried the sleeping man through. Mere passage through the gates was enough for the iron to work its damage on them; all cried out as the fiery cold of the iron leapt upon their skin.

At the sound of their wails, the man stirred, lolling his head from side to side. For just a moment, his eyes flickered open, catching sight of the queen's face. He didn't wake, but it was enough. He fell back into his slumber, but for that brief moment, he had seen.

The servants set him down on the other side of the gates, and their wild eyes pleaded with the queen. With her blistered hands, still stinging from the iron's bite, she called forth a wind that whipped around them. It lashed their faces—their feathered and furred faces—until all the fire was put out.

The queen laughed. She felt better than she had in ages. The man still slept under an enchantment, but she knew it could be broken. Hadn't she met his eyes with her own? With light steps, she led the way to the heart of Illvelion.

Gallien had slowed his steps. Morning was approaching and with it the light of the sun. For now, all was still gray, but the stars were beginning to fade.

The ground around them was muddy and uneven.

Everywhere they looked trees lay broken and uprooted, victims of the mudslide from the Mud Lord's fallen city. Clay and sludge blanketed the forest floor. Gwen hardly looked; she didn't want to be reminded.

Something caught the unicorn's eye because he suddenly stopped and shifted directions, heading further south instead of southeast. Tom, and then even Gwen, saw it too: a glint of iron. It caught the first beams of sunrise. Gallien pawed at the mud and uncovered a heavy iron chain, buried in the sludge. The chain looked like a dead snake, carried through the cascading mud like a piece of flotsam.

"What is this, I wonder?" said the unicorn, but something in his voice told Gwen that he knew exactly what it was. He nudged it with his hoof.

"I—" Gwen began, but Gallien didn't wait for her to finish. He trampled the iron chain, pounding it into the ground. Mud sprayed everywhere, coating the glistening flank of the unicorn with dark streaks. A few flecks landed on the hem of Gwen's dress. They looked like dried worms on pale stone. Still, the unicorn kept stomping on the iron chain. Gwen thought she saw sparks fly as Gallien danced. The sun rose above the horizon like a flaming coin.

When at last he lifted his hooves, there were deep indents in the mud where the chain had been, but no trace of it remained except for one dull glint sticking out of the sodden earth.

"I will lower myself so that you may dismount," Gallien said. "Gwenhivar, take what is rightfully yours."

She hesitated to press her feet into the mud, as if the clay might swallow her up for her transgressions against it. But instead, she stood firm on the wet earth and bent to pick up the thing which the unicorn had hammered. It was cold in her hand, fitting just right in her palm, but it burned when she held it, and when the pain shot through her arm, she felt her body suddenly filled with a dense fog. Despite the pain and the dampening, Gwen did not drop the ironwork. She looked at it with a sort of resignation and then held it up for the others to see.

The iron key was heavy in her hand, and it still burned cold, but the pain was beginning to dull, or she was beginning to acquiesce to it. "What does it lock?" she said.

"Or open?" said Tom, hopefully. He stared a bit wide-eyed at the key which had once been a chain as long as a man.

"The way to the queen," answered Gallien. He said no more, and neither Tom nor Gwen pressed him. They thought only of the magic which had made the chain to the key.

Gwen knew she couldn't keep holding it, for, despite her resolve, the cold of the iron still ached on her skin. She pressed the key into one of her pockets and felt her hand relax.

"My father had the good sense to insist on pockets for my dresses," she said, trying to break the strange solemnity of the moment. But it was no use. She swooned. She clutched her side. She began to fall to her knees.

"Gwen!" Tom clattered down from Gallien's back. He went to her.

"She hungers," said Gallien, unperturbed. "The body still marks its human frailty."

"Yes," Gwen replied, "I can't remember when

last I've eaten." The swoon had passed, but she still looked ashen. Tom, too, had eyes wide with hunger. His face went eagerly to Gallien's. The unicorn nodded and sauntered off.

"Do you think he can find anything in all this wreckage?" said Gwen. She and Tom had found a place to rest under a large ash tree where the mud wasn't as thick. They felt the warming sunlight on their skin.

"If anyone can, it's him," said Tom. "I hope."

They sat in silence for a long while, their hunger gnawing away at their courage. At last, Tom swallowed his worries and spoke.

"Your father sounds like a good fellow. Thinking of the little things for you." He indicated her pockets.

"What? Oh, yes. I suppose so. I—" she stumbled over the next word and then thought better of it.

Their silence returned. Tom hung his head down a bit, and Gwen thought it was his stomach aching, but when she looked again, she saw the shining wetness of tears in his eyes.

"You look so human," Gwen said, almost to herself. Her fingers stretched out to touch his sandy hair. She meant it for comfort. "How did your curse befall you?"

Tom made himself smaller, shrinking away from her.

"I'm sorry, that wasn't fair," Gwen said. "You don't owe me such answers."

Tom's voice was muffled, diminished. "You can ask me. It's just—" He snuffled and wiped his nose on his sleeve. "I don't know. Can't remember."

"But if you can't remember, then how do you know it was a curse?" Gwen didn't know why she blurted that out; she couldn't help it. Her curiosity overruled her paltry compassion.

Tom's eyes flashed hot. "I don't need to remember! I just know!"

It was Gwen's turn to shrink away. "I'm sorry. But you just look..." She swallowed the rest.

"I look it, aye. But then what about you? You look it too, but what are you? With your spell inside and the power to move the earth? You're not so human either!"

Gwen shivered. The evidence of her power was all around them. Mud and clay and ruin.

They sat in silence again and both wished the unicorn would return. Their stomachs ached.

But when the sun climbed higher overhead, still, Gallien did not return. Tom stood up to stretch even though it took all of his strength. He sat back down close to Gwen.

"Can I ask you," he began, "why you came back for me? You could've gone on to find the queen yourself instead of turning 'round and plucking me from the Mud Lord."

"What kind of partner would I be if I had left you to such a fate?"

"A false partner, aye." Tom hung his head a little. "But you have been true."

"You as well," said Gwen. "You didn't have to help me in the first place. Yes, I know you think the queen can lift your curse, but even still, you needn't have brought me along. You needn't have bothered."

Tom didn't answer.

"I suppose neither of us likes to be alone," Gwen said.

The sun sweltered and the shadow of the ash tree

grew shorter. All around them the mud baked into hardened clay. A dry, burnt smell wafted through the air.

"Oh, when will he come!" Gwen sighed. She clutched her stomach.

Tom said nothing. Both children worried the worst. Gallien was a strange one; there was no telling if he was a true friend or foe.

"If we must," said Gwen, finally, "we will find our own way. Surely you can find berries or roots or something edible."

Tom grimaced. "I might, but I don't know this realm well. And even so..."

Gwen understood. What was there to find in this wasteland? The question hung in her mind like a dark shadow. What *was* there to find here? Her father? Was she clinging to a false hope, to a phantom long since vanished? How could she ever find him in this strange and bleak place, even if the queen granted her favor? What would she do when the quest proved fruitless?

The thought pierced her like a spear-point. She was a child cursed, something other than human, something with a spell and fairy power churning inside her. How could she ever go back over the edge of the forest and return to her world?

"If the queen breaks your curse," Gwen said suddenly, "where will you go?"

"I don't know."

Gwen's temper flared. Tom wasn't being forthright. She could see the distracted look in his glassy eyes. "You're not being honest."

"I am," said Tom. "I am." He said this last with a bitter tongue.

"What I mean is, where is your home?" Gwen tried again.

Tom just shook his head. "She won't break the curse."

"But why?"

Before Tom could answer, they both heard the heavy footfalls of Gallien. He carried something grayish-yellow in his teeth.

"They will taste of rainwater and dirt, but they will sustain you," he told the children. He dropped them to the ground and the children could see they were mushrooms.

Gwen looked at the swelling, sickly flesh of the fungi and recoiled. She knew this kind and had always been told by her father they were poisonous.

Seeing her fear, Gallien snorted. A kind of laugh. "You are part of Faerie now, child. These will not hurt you."

Gwen swallowed the truth. She couldn't deny it. More than the power to move mud and earth, the power to eat that which would poison told her the transformation was real. She could not go home again.

She and Tom ate greedily. The mushrooms had a foul taste, but as soon as they swallowed them, their hunger pangs subsided.

"Let us go," said the unicorn. "The wind tells me the queen is deep in her abode, but for how long, we cannot know. Haste!"

They climbed upon his back once more and set off. Mud sprayed up from his beating hooves, but Gallien's speed was so great that soon they left the wastelands of the Mud Lord behind, heading toward a dense part of the forest, filled with towering oaks.

Their pace slowed. Gwen wondered if the trees here were too thick for Gallien to navigate, but then she considered how lithe and water-like he was, and decided he had slowed for another reason. Surely, he could gallop where he willed.

"Why have you slowed?" she asked, boldly.

"Tom," Gallien replied, "we are near an old friend of yours."

Tom's body went rigid.

"Shall we stop and offer greetings?" the unicorn continued.

Tom shook his head wildly. "No! Let's go around! Please, Gallien..."

"As you wish. He may not be at home, after all. Out searching."

"For you, Tom?" Gwen interrupted. "Your wood grue friend?"

"The very same," answered Gallien.

"He's no friend," said Tom, darkly.

Gwen felt Tom squirm behind her. "But you were going to take me to him," she said. "Now you speak of him so bitterly?"

Tom had no answer.

"It is best we avoid him," said Gallien at last. "He can do us no help."

Gwen thought this all very strange. Her companions spoke as if they knew some secret, and she wanted to know what. But Gallien's words weighed heavily in the air, so she held her tongue.

❧

The queen watched from her window as the stars faded in the morning light. Dawn approached, and she grew weary. Many hours ago her bed had been prepared by the servants, but she had not rested. The man whom she had claimed slept on a satin couch nearby, his sleep a death-like silence that was not aroused by any spell she had yet tried. Now she was ready for her own sleep, but she could not bring herself to lie down. She needed this man to awaken, to see his eyes look upon her. Her magic was not what it once was; her powers were failing just at the moment when she wanted them most. All other times and seasons when her magic had flourished seemed as chaff to her now. Now she wanted a spell that could awaken this man who filled her every thought and dream.

She looked at him again. He had more life in him even in sleep than she had in herself. His face, though pale, was fired from within by his human soul. She loved that fire, and she craved it for herself. *But—*

The thought stole into her mind and pained her. *No.* She could not. If she did, perhaps the very thing she loved would be lost. But if she did not, then he might sleep forever and would be as good as dead to her.

The queen turned back to her window and watched the sunrise. The light from it hit her face and reminded her of how translucent and thin her skin had become over the years. The sun's beams pierced right through her.

She called to her servant, a small furry creature with a face like a root. "Take his sword," she commanded. "Melt it down and mix it with silver, and fashion a goblet worthy of a king."

Looking once more upon the man's face, the

queen sighed. His countenance would change, and so would his heart, but she was willing to pay such a price for the sake of his company.

CHAPTER SEVEN

OAK ABODE

Snuffling like a pig, he kept his thin nose to the spongy ground. They were near; he could smell them. Near enough to leave a scent. Human stink. But they had changed directions. Away from him. Away. Little runt must have known. Betrayed him, he has. Betrayed.

Alas, it would be hard to catch them. They were going swift. Thorn could tell. Had help, they did. A swift friend. But Thorn could be patient. He could wait. They would need to rest soon. All creatures need rest, even the swiftest. And Thorn would keep sniffing them out. Sniffing until he'd found his prizes.

The trees were dense, blocking out the light. Their foliage spread across the sky making an endless green canopy. An oak leaf floated down after a light breeze, and Gwen was surprised to see that it was as big as her head. Like so much of this forest, everywhere she looked was bereft of fauna. No squirrels danced from branch to branch, no rabbits darted through the undergrowth. Even insects were missing. Only the trees and the soil. At least there was no more mud here.

"We are nearer," said Gallien, sensing the question that was rising to Gwen's lips. "But the queen will not let us pass unchallenged."

"If it's too dangerous..." Tom began, looking pale.

Gwen noticed that Tom had been strangely silent these past few hours. Ever since Gallien had mentioned the wood grue, Tom had said nothing, made no sound. She thought it was due to exhaustion or the harrowing moments of the past few days, but now she heard his voice quiver.

"Finding the queen always entails danger," said Gallien, nonplussed.

"Maybe there's another way," squeaked Tom. "Safer."

Gallien whinnied his sharp, high laugh. "How long have you lived in the forest, little puck? You should know there is no safety here."

"Come now, Tom," said Gwen, "don't you want the queen to break your curse?"

Tom mumbled, "What if she wants something else?"

"You are on the path," replied Gallien. "To turn back would be the coward's way."

"What about another rest, Gallien?" asked Gwen. "Perhaps Tom is tired. I know I am. We've been riding for days, it seems."

"Only a few hours, human child," said the unicorn, shaking his head.

"Really? It feels like ages."

"You are not used to such swiftness, I think."

"What about it, Gallien? May we rest?" Gwen urged. "These oaks are beautifully strange. Such huge leaves!"

"Hmm," began Gallien. "They may be beautiful, but I am not sure who inhabits this grove."

They needed to eat again, so Gallien went off to search. But Gwen was still captivated by the magnificent oak leaves. They continued to fall at odd times, sometimes when a light breeze blew but sometimes not. And they were fresh and green, not the leaves of dying autumn. She started to gather them up, placing them into a stack like pieces of parchment.

"How lovely!" she exclaimed. "Look, Tom, look! Aren't they beautiful?"

"They're leaves, I suppose." He still looked pale and sick. "Listen, I don't think... I mean, maybe don't go to the queen..."

Gwen cut him off. "They look good enough to eat!" She was still caressing the pile of enormous leaves gathered in her lap.

This stopped Tom's stammering. "Eat? Can humans eat oak leaves?"

Gwen didn't answer. She bent her head down into the leaves and breathed in their smell. They were more fragrant than any leaves she could remember back home in Estline. They smelled of fresh wood and rainwater and the sun. There was something else too, something sweet and almost perfume-like. She breathed in their scent again.

Tom stood up and looked around the wood. No other leaves fell amongst the trees except the one where they were resting. The air was still calm, with only the merest hint of a breeze.

"We should look for Gallien," he said, but Gwen didn't listen. Her head drooped over the leaves resting gently in her lap. Her eyes were dim.

Tom looked around again. Something was amiss, but he couldn't see it. A speck of movement in the distance, then nothing. A feeling of eyes watching, but no one there. Gwen was groggy now, not thinking straight. She clutched the leaves against her chest and sucked in their scent. Swooning, her eyes dimmed as if to pass out, but Tom rushed to her and swatted the leaves away as best he could. He pulled her up to her feet.

"Come on! We're going to find Gallien!"

Gwen stumbled, dazed. Tom dragged her along. As they went, more leaves drifted down around them. Tom could smell their sweetness now too, and it took all his willpower to ignore the scent. It was unnatural, all these green leaves falling to the forest floor like it was autumn. He called for Gallien as Gwen wandered somnolently behind him. No answer came from any direction, only the ruffle of falling leaves.

They did smell fragrant. Tom had never smelled oak leaves like these before. There was some enchantment here, he knew it now, and all he could think was that they needed Gallien to help them. With his human curse laid upon him, Tom had no way of stopping the enchantment. But the unicorn might. Even Gwen might, Tom realized. But she was already sleepwalking behind him.

He found Gallien not far away. Oak leaves covered the great, gleaming body like a blanket. The unicorn was lying on his side, eyes closed, unmoving. The scent here was strongest, and Tom couldn't stop himself from breathing it in. It made him feel warm inside—comforted, like being in his mother's arms—a feeling that he couldn't remember ever having felt before. His eyes drooped with contentment, with resignation.

"Aye, little runt," a voice said, hard and rough like sandpaper. "Take your medicine and don't fight back." A horn blew and more leaves fell.

Tom's sight grew dark; everything around him faded. But before he slept, he saw something familiar: the glimpse of a face, wretched and cruel, and fingers rough as bark reaching to catch him.

Twilight was drawing near, and still, her servants worked at their craft. The queen was anxious for the goblet to be finished, but she could wait a little while longer. She had waited this long to find someone like the man who slept next to her; she could wait a few more hours or even days. She had stayed in her room all day, watching the hours pass outside her window, watching the man sleep, trying to remember.

There were things that flashed inside her mind that disturbed her. Another kingdom, a dew-drenched lawn, the edge of a dark forest that called to her in her grief. And a baby's laughter. It hurt her to think of it. The laughter gave her no pleasure.

Slowly, her eyes dimmed. Sleep, at long last, came upon her. She rested by the window, unable to even stumble to her canopied bed. Her arm touched the cold glass as she lay her head down on the sill. Dreams wouldn't come. The sleep was dark. Voices came instead, muffled and red.

"She has forbidden us."

"Yet we come."

Laughter. Cruel laughter.

"Shall we wake her?"

"We shall. She shall know her power is waning." The fingernail of the last fairy reached out and traced a thin scratch on the queen's cheek. Her eyes fluttered open at the scratch and saw the three fairies leering at her, crowding around the windowsill.

Like a hound, she sprung up in defense, her body rigid. For a long, silent moment, neither she nor the fairies spoke. The queen knew their presence meant her powers were indeed weakening, for the gates and the spells woven around her inner kingdom had been made to keep these three and their kindred out.

"Yes," said the red one, groping towards her with its eyeless form. "Yes, we come despite your attempts to forestall."

"And who does the queen have here?" said the last one, turning towards the sleeping man. "A former feast? Hope to regain what was lost?"

"Stay back," the queen commanded, her voice an utter coldness. "Our parlays are done. Our business finished long ago."

"We have new business," said the dark one. "You stole him." The shadow crept toward the man in his enchanted sleep.

"I still have power here," the queen threatened. She raised a hand and the fire of the setting sun blazed through the room. The dark fairy recoiled, afraid of the light.

The last fairy, its bulbous eyes gleaming in the light's glow, laughed. "Your power! All that you have has been given to you. What power do you have that we cannot counter?"

"I kept you at bay this long, didn't I?" the queen returned. "I will find a way to banish you again."

"But for what?" hissed the red fairy. "We like you. And our bargains." It groped toward her and fumbled at the hem of her dress.

The queen did not move. She stood as still as an ancient oak.

"We will not feast on your human pet," said the last one. "But we want—"

All three fairies froze.

The queen stepped back, wide-eyed, wondering what had happened.

The fairies looked at each other, and then, like dry leaves blown away in a gusting wind, they fled from the room, back through the window, out into the air.

The queen didn't allow herself to relax. Her spells were failing. It was only a matter of time until her enemies returned and perhaps even brought with them something worse. She needed to prepare. Though she longed to stay with the man who slept so peacefully, she knew that he too would be threatened if the old ones returned or sent their cruel servants to ravage her kingdom.

With one last glance at his gentle face, the queen hurried from the room to begin the long work of saving her kingdom.

❧

"Little Tom's been bad," said the wood grue, shaking the boy out of his stupor. "Lazy wretch."

Tom couldn't see at first; his eyes were crusted over with a deep slumber. But soon his lids peeled back and light filled them. It was a dull, greenish light. The light of Thorn's lanterns. Filled with oil crushed out of beetles and mixed with the paste of acorn meat, the lanterns burned low and barely illuminated. Here was Thorn's den, a hollow oak, stinking of rotten bark and home to worms and dark crawling things. Tom must have dreamed it all: the human girl, the mud gnomes, the unicorn. Here was his old home, though it had never been much of one. A home for toil and servitude.

"Get up!" Thorn scolded again. Tom felt a bucket shoved into his hand. It was empty but stunk of sulfur from all the muck and bug carcasses that had filled it over the years. Tom's chores awaited. Cleaning the storerooms, patching the holes in the rotten bark, carting out the dead beetles and crawlers that were no longer of use.

He sighed and got up. As Thorn moved away, Tom caught only a glimpse of his master. The wood grue was never in one spot for long; always moving out of the corner of one's eye, he couldn't be seen clearly. Only glimpses: a patch of matted fur, long fingers made of bark, eyes as dark as river pebbles. Tom would see his master in a flash, and then the wood grue would be gone, moved to some other corner, just out of sight. But the voice was unmistakable: rough and cold, not a hint of kindness.

"That's right," said Thorn, "get to work."

Tom shuffled off into the deep storerooms of the house. He felt the weight of his servitude sink into his shoulders. This life was such a burden, but with his wretched curse—his human form—Thorn said it was all Tom was good for. If only he could find that human child. Thorn had told him a human child had been spotted in the woods, and that the queen had wanted it. If they could bring it to her, she might reward them. Tom's curse could be lifted, his need to stay with Thorn would be gone. But hadn't he already found the child? Hadn't he already planned to take her to the queen himself?

Tom's head was foggy. The storerooms were overflowing with desiccated beetles and spiders. It looked as if Thorn hadn't emptied them in weeks. Images of a golden-haired girl flitted through Tom's mind as he scooped the bugs into his bucket. She had a sapphire dress that was faded at the hem and eyes that shifted from bright blue to cloudy grey, but the more Tom tried to picture her, the more his head grew heavy and began to hurt.

He knew he should tell Thorn what he might have found. Thorn would want to know about the girl. Hadn't his master said the queen would be angry if they didn't bring her a human child? But Tom held his tongue and tried to concentrate on his work. He remembered what Thorn had said about the queen, what she wanted for the child. He shuddered.

"Oi! Runt! Bring me my meal!" Thorn's voice echoed through the dark depths of the oak tree. "Better set the plates for four," Thorn continued as Tom carried in a bucket of black worms and millipedes and set it near the crude table in the center of Thorn's sitting room.

Everything about Thorn's home was off-kilter in some way. The tables were always crooked, with one leg shorter than the rest; the chairs were slanted down so it was hard to stay on them. Bowls and cups and plates were all malformed so that food or drink slopped out of them and spilled. Tom, of course, would be tasked with cleaning up the mess.

The dull green light of the lanterns made sure to keep Thorn's face in shadow, and he bustled about the room, looking through various cracks in the bark walls, watching and waiting for something.

"Not here yet," he muttered. "Making me wait. Looking down their noses at old Thorn, I'd wager."

"Who is making you wait?" Tom asked. Although Thorn was often cruel, the one thing he allowed Tom to do was to ask questions.

"The envoys," Thorn answered. "Come to take the girl to the queen."

Tom's stomach sank. *The girl.* She wasn't a dream after all. He felt his head spin as he looked around the room, both frantic and terrified to find her. But there was no girl, only Thorn's musty hovel.

"Thought you could take her to the queen yerself, I know," grumbled Thorn. "Trying to step out on me. But old Thorn is craftier than that. Where are they?" He scurried to look out the door, his body a furry shadow to Tom's eyes. "Keeping me waiting."

Thorn allowed Tom to ask questions, but the one on his lips now hung nervously. He set the bucket of slop on the table and propped a wobbly plate underneath to keep it from slipping to the floor. He looked again around the room but saw no sign of the human child. Perhaps she was hidden in one of the storerooms. But Tom had just been inside clearing out the refuse. Maybe Thorn's magic was greater than Tom had realized. Fleeting visions of the oak forest and the fragrant leaves flashed through his mind. Whatever spell had fogged his memory had been powerful, something Tom had never seen his master do before.

"It worked," said Thorn to the unseen guests. They had arrived, silent as owl wings.

Tom, instinctively, slunk away from the room into the shadows of the hallway.

"Where is our prize?" hissed a voice that sounded like darkness given form.

"Show us our new ward," said another voice, red as a holly berry.

Thorn stepped aside grandly and waved the voices to his table. Tom had never seen such creatures, but he knew them right away. They were the old things that dwell in the heart of the forest. The devourers. The powers that lay hidden, rulers of a deeper realm.

"I need payment first," growled Thorn, unfazed by these dangerous guests. "Eat at my table, drink of my drink, pay what you owe. Then I'll show you the human whelp."

"We traveled far for this child," growled the dark voice.

"And abandoned our audience with the queen," said the red.

"Our haste here shall not be in vain," said the last voice of the three. "But come, let us oblige this meager creature, if he insists."

The other two voices groaned but did as they were told. They slurped up the bowls of millipedes and drank stale rainwater, then they let their bowls and cups rattle on the table. The empty vessels slid to the floor.

"Tom! Clean the mess!" said Thorn.

Tom had no choice but to come back into the room, but he kept his head down and eyes averted from the faces of the three old ones.

"Another human?" whispered the red one. "Do you offer this as well, wood grue?"

"Not a real human. A curse. This lad is truly a puck." Thorn's voice had an edge to it. *Fear*, Tom thought.

The old ones kept their gazes fixed upon the boy.

"And in service to me," Thorn added hastily.

"Well then," said the last voice slowly, "show us the real one. No more delay."

Thorn motioned for the others to follow him. Out they went from the oak tree into the twilight shadows.

Tom cleared the bowls and cups as fast as he could, throwing them into his slop-filled bucket, and then he followed Thorn and the old ones into the night air. He moved carefully, silent as the tread of a sparrow on the grass, keeping a fair distance. But he could see the others up ahead, moving into the brambles that surrounded Thorn's tree. Soon the branches were pulled back to reveal a pale girl in a faded dress of sapphire, her eyes closed, her face still. The three old ones curled around her, obscuring her from Tom's sight.

"Our partnership is renewed," said the red voice, leaning over the girl.

"Eh?" Thorn replied, eager. "Partnership?"

"Not with you!" the dark voice cried.

"With her," whispered the last one, but Tom could hear it like an echo, resounding off the trees.

"Will the queen be pleased?" Thorn said, that hint of fear creeping back in. "Pay my due. If she be pleased, then pay up."

The three old ones laughed, and with grasping

fingers, they plucked the girl from her bed of brambles.

Up into the air, they flew, like a smoke of black and red, twisted with faded blue, leaving Thorn behind, empty-handed. The wood grue raged at the sky, but all that answered were the fluttering oak leaves.

Gwen.

That had been her name. Tom remembered it all now. As he stood there remembering, lost in revelry, he did not see Thorn approach, the anger swelling in his face. If Tom had looked, he would have seen the wood grue in full—no more glimpses or quick movements—stalking towards him with wrath. Instead, Tom remembered how Gwen had saved him from the prison of the Mud Lord, and her power. And he remembered Gallien, and wondered if the unicorn might still save the girl or if she was now lost forever to the old ones and the queen.

"Betrayed!" cried Thorn. "Took her without payment! And you—" he leaped at Tom, a flurry of sharp wooden fingers cutting into Tom's skin "—you helped them! Kept her from me! They already knew her! Betrayed!"

Tom cowered as best he could. He hadn't felt Thorn's wickedness in a long time, but he always remembered its threat. When he'd first been pressed into service, those bark claws had scratched his human skin, shown him his place. He had remembered ever since not to cross his master.

"Get home!" Thorn spat, his body slumped and heaving from the effort of his attack. "Get to work. Fill my buckets with all you can find in-store. We are leaving, you and I. Find the queen ourselves, get my reward." He shuffled off to gather acorns.

Tom winced in pain and did not watch his master leave. The cuts were not deep but they stung like fire and made his body ache.

For a quick moment, Tom thought of running away. No geas or enchantment kept him here, no chain or lock. Only fear. Thorn wasn't looking, all Tom needed to do was...

No. It would not work. The wood grue would find him, just as he had found Tom and Gwen and Gallien earlier.

Tom wondered about the unicorn. Was he looking for them? If he could find Gallien himself, then he might have a chance. Even Thorn could not outrun a unicorn.

But what of Gwen? She had been taken, carried off to the queen. Tom's heart stung to think of it. The queen, who hates all humans and would do worse things still to the child. Tom cursed himself for saying nothing, for leading Gwen into a falsehood, for thinking of his own skin instead. She had trusted him, and he had tricked her. Now she was to suffer for his lies.

Thorn was nowhere in sight. Tom's mind started to race again, the thoughts forming into plans. If he, Tom, could get there first...

The moon had risen, full and bright. Amongst the brambles, a dull glint caught Tom's eyes. Lying in the dirt was something small and silver-gray. He reached for it, feeling the coldness before his skin even touched it.

Gwen's key.

It burned his skin to touch it, but he put it in his

pocket quickly and the burning subsided. He could feel it throbbing against his leg, but it was bearable. The weight of it was startling, though. Tom thought he might not be able to even walk with such a weight pulling him down. But he knew he must. It was his fault that Gwen was now in the hands of the old ones. He lifted a foot, told himself to run. He didn't look where he was going...

The face of Thorn filled his vision. No more glimpses, no more flashes in the corner of his eye. The full form of the wood grue was there, rushing upon him, illuminated by the moon's light.

"Thief!" cried Thorn, sharp fingers extended, black eyes gleaming. Tom didn't even know what was happening. All he saw was Thorn—all of Thorn —like a hungry rat, leaping towards him. Their eyes met. Thorn realized it too late.

The body of the wood grue sucked inward, constricting into itself, and then, as quick as a blink, what flesh and bone were inside the matted fur of the creature vanished, leaving behind only a grayish pelt of fur and bark. A harsh scream echoed across the treetops and was gone. The lifeless pelt fell to the ground with a dull thud.

Tom closed his eyes, hoping to unsee what had just happened. To watch a living thing dissolve into a pile of skin and fur, all in an instant, was too much to bear. It was Tom's look that had done it: a gaze without obscurity or veil or periphery. The wood grue could not abide such a gaze. It had destroyed him. Tom shivered.

Had it always been this way? Was this Thorn's weakness? Or was something different now for Tom? Strange powers were shifting through the world.

Hadn't Gwen turned the earth upside down in the mud cliffs?

Tom shook his head and opened his eyes. He made himself look at the pile of fur that had once been Thorn. He couldn't waste any more time on fears and regrets. Gwen would soon be in the hands of the queen. It was his fault. His lies. He needed to get there before she did.

Something stopped him. The skin of Thorn lay at his feet like a deflated sack. He considered it. What would happen when he came to the gates of the queen? What would happen to a puck who looked human?

It was the last thing he wanted to do, but Tom had no choice. He had to make things right. He had shaken her hand and promised—a false promise then, but a true promise now. He couldn't let the queen have her.

Slowly, Tom bent down and picked up the pile of matted fur and weathered skin that had once been his cruel master. It hung down heavy in his hands, a quilt of wet rags. He sighed, closed his eyes, and pulled the skin over his head.

CHAPTER EIGHT

AGRAVAINE'S CURSE

"It is finished," they said in hushed voices. But the queen was not in her chamber. The servants whispered among themselves, wondering where she had gone. The goblet was made; it was ready for her spells. But without the queen, the servants did not know what to do. They set the goblet down next to the sleeping man and shuffled out.

No one knew where the queen had gone. Some had seen her hurry down the halls at twilight, but no one knew her purpose. All began to whisper and wonder: was the queen, at last, afraid? Rumor spread that her magic was weakening, and all of them quivered to think what would happen next. Perhaps the sleeping man would wake up, and they would have a new sovereign.

Deep in the golden woods of Illvelion's dells, the queen wandered. She had searched through the night but found nothing that would help her. These woods were where she had found her first spell, and it was here, she thought, where she might find something more to renew her power. But there was nothing. No herbs to eat, no flowers to crush and mix in a draught.

No water even to drink. The streams that had flowed through here once were all gone: dried up or disappeared. She had forgotten how much this place could change without warning.

"I'm a fool," she said. She knew where her real power had come from and it wasn't in these small weeds. But the ones who had made her had flown away, had rushed from her presence to some other errand. She wasn't sad to see them gone. What she needed was not more of their bargains, or some hedge magic lifted from the forest floor. She needed a greater power. Something to make her more than she once was.

"Gallien."

The unicorn stood before the queen, his appearance as sudden as the first raindrop before a storm.

"M'lady," said the unicorn, bowing his head. "If I can tread unhindered in these woods, then others may as well."

"They already have," replied the queen. "Come and gone, but don't think I mistook their meaning."

"They will come again. They have found a new ward. Like unto yourself, I should say."

The queen had not expected this. She hungered to ask Gallien what he meant. "All the more reason for strengthening my realm against intrusion."

"Think you shall?"

"There is a way," the queen said, eyeing the unicorn closely.

"You will not learn the secret from me. You are a stranger here, despite your crown."

"You want the old ones to prevail?"

"I didn't say that."

"Then tell me! The sea foam bird! How may I call it?"

Gallien snorted and pawed at the ground. "You would ask that? What fearsome magics do you intend?"

"Only to stop those who would reclaim my kingdom and feed upon the land. You say they have a new ward. I must prevent it."

"You might not think so when you meet her."

"Her?" The queen tried to keep her voice steady. "What purpose brought you here, Gallien? It was not to aid me."

"You mistake me, m'lady. I did not come as an enemy."

"As a friend?" The queen scoffed.

"What you intend, I cannot abide. Leave the white bird alone. Find some other way."

"Some other way? Spilt blood is the only magic strong enough."

Gallien did not reply. His body glistened in the morning sunlight. His horn shone like a gilded blade, casting a blinding gleam into the queen's eyes. She shielded herself from the glare, and in the darkness behind her closed lids, she saw what must be done. It was as clear to her as the waters of the glass pool. She opened her eyes. The light had dimmed a little, the sun's rays hiding behind the treetops. Gallien stood before her like a marble statue.

"So be it," said the queen. Her fingers clenched into fists, her throat moaned. The wind gathered above her, flinging the treetops back and forth like dry grass. Her eyes gazed up at the gathering tempest, then they cast their sight at Gallien. Quicker than a knife, the wind cut. The unicorn screamed. Golden light coated the air like blood. Hooves reared up—a cry in the blinding whiteness—then a terrible thud.

The forest dimmed as the golden light faded. Gallien lay on the ground, panting heavily. He was the color of driftwood. His forehead was marred. Where the horn had been was now only a stump, the face of it smooth as polished glass.

At the feet of the queen was the horn, pulsing dully with dim light. She picked it up and turned to go. Gallien's breathing slowed to a faint wheeze. He closed his eyes, but the queen did not see. She had already left the forest.

Tom cursed himself for a fool. He had no idea how to find the queen. Setting off in haste, he hadn't reckoned with his directionless plan. To head west and try to find the hidden pool would take too long, and with Thorn dead, he had no one to ask where the queen's inner kingdom was. The old ones and Gwen would be there long before he could even find directions. He wandered through the forest anyway, desperate for his luck to help him, but deep down he knew relying on luck was mere foolishness. Wearing Thorn's skin, he had felt himself transform into the visage of the wood grue, but even still, he could feel the eyes of the forest averting their gaze and hiding from him. Perhaps they feared Thorn's wrath. In any case, Tom couldn't find anyone to help him.

The iron key in his pocket throbbed at times, stinging his leg with a burning cold. But then the cold would subside and Tom forgot about it. As the sun crested over the horizon, he looked for some sign that might point in the right direction, but all he saw were more and more trees. He trudged for a little way longer, and as he did, the iron key pulsed quicker. His leg began to ache. He had to sit down and rest, and when he did, the key's biting cold subsided. He had been walking all night and now his eyes grew heavy. But Tom resisted sleep. There was danger in sleep. He did the only thing he could think of as his eyes dimmed: he took out the key and let it sting his hand.

The pain was dull but enough to clear his mind. He squeeze the ice-cold iron until the desire for sleep subsided, then, when the pain was growing too strong, he let the key drop from his hand. It landed on the ground with a thud heavier than its small size. Tom looked at his hand and was surprised to see not a single mark or singe of the flesh.

He sighed. He wasn't any closer to finding the queen or knowing the way. His head was cleared of sleep, but he was no clearer on what to do. He bent to pick up the key again. But when he reached for it, he jumped back. The key had begun to spin, twirling back and forth like a needle in a compass. Tom stared at it, disbelieving. There was no wind to make it move, no earth quaking. There was no one in the woods nearby to cast a spell on it. The key swung from side to side, then spun quickly, then slowed again. It was searching.

At last, it stopped, pointing out a direction. The sun was still in the morning sky and the key pointed toward it. East. Carefully, Tom reached down and took the key back into his hand. Its coldness seeped through Thorn's skin into his own, but he didn't drop it again. He held it in his palm and let it point the way. As he walked toward the sun, the key's iron sting throbbed more intensely. Tom took it for a sign.

&

The raven with swollen goblin toes rapped its beak on the queen's chamber door. "Majesty," it croaked, "there is a stranger at the gates. A wood grue."

The goblet and the unicorn horn sat on a table near her bedside. The queen had done nothing with either object since returning. The man who slept was still beside her, deep in his enchantment. The queen hoped that he would wake up without need of the goblet—a desperate hope, she knew—but no words or tinctures or touch could rouse him. A crystal pitcher of clear rainwater had been brought by her servants; the goblet waited to be filled. The queen hesitated.

"Majesty," the raven repeated.

A deep sickness ran through her, the queen now knew. It caused her magic to wither; it made her heart grow faint. Why could she not take the goblet and make the man drink? She felt again the cold wind that had cut off the unicorn's horn; it made her skin crawl. But the wind bit only against her mind: a figment of guilt.

She had lost something long ago. Perhaps it had been herself that was lost; she couldn't be sure. Something in the man's face, in the strands of hair that fell across his forehead, made her think she could recover it, but the sickness was too deep. If she filled the goblet now and gave him drink, if she put a spell inside him...

"A stranger, your majesty," said the raven, its voice strained. "A wood grue."

The queen shook herself out of her dark thoughts. "The gates will keep him out. A wood grue is too weak to break through."

"He has a key, majesty."

A key? At first, the queen did not understand. There was no key to the iron gates. But fear seized her and the thought of the three fairies and their new ward overcame her. Was this their aim, to make a key that would unlock all the queen's power? A key that even a common wood grue could use against her?

Burying any thought of sickness or grief, she seized the unicorn horn and went to the window. She channeled her will into the glimmering horn, and with a thought, gathered the clouds overhead so that they swirled a marble gray. Thunder shook the earth and rain pelted the grass. Lightning split the sky.

The raven jumped up on the windowsill. "Still he comes!" it croaked. "The key has opened the gates!"

Furious, the queen swept the raven aside and raised the horn toward the storm clouds. She cried out, and a clap of thunder rattled the very foundations of her castle. A dozen bolts of lightning speared the ground at once, and the wind uprooted trees, but still, it was no use. The wood grue continued to crawl toward the queen.

She turned to the goblet. She had resisted, but no longer. Filling it with water, the queen watched as the liquid began to shimmer like quicksilver in the goblet's bowl. She lifted it to the sleeping man's lips. A few drops fell into his mouth, and he swallowed.

His eyelids fluttered as he mumbled, then he awoke. He took one moment to see everything in the room: the queen, her servant, the fine things within her chamber. As the queen leaned forward, he recoiled, disoriented fear filling his face. But then the spell began to work, writhing its way within him, and the fear and uncertainty and everything previous melted away, leaving the man serene.

"I came looking for someone," he said. "But I can't remember who."

"Perhaps for me," the queen replied. She dared to approach him, and he did not flinch. Touching his arm, she smiled. "I have need of you."

His eyes were glassy and distant, but he seemed to understand. He looked at her with that serene expression and nodded.

"What do they call you?" she asked. Somewhere in her memory, the queen was dancing around a sound or a name that felt familiar, but it was a memory that eluded her.

He hesitated, his face coloring in shame. "I do not remember."

The queen hid her disappointment. "What we are called is less important than what we do," she said, ignoring her guilt. "Will you help me?"

The man's posture straightened as if he had just now realized he had a body that was thick with muscle and strength.

The queen held out the unicorn horn. "This. Take it. An intruder has charmed his way into my kingdom. Drive him back. My servant will show you the way."

The man vacillated again back to uncertainty, his eyes distant. But the queen forced the horn into his hands, and when he held it, he gripped it firmly. His eyes flashed with streaks of fire. He did not remember much, but he knew what to do with a weapon in his hand.

♨

Tom put the key back into his pocket, hidden under the folds of Thorn's skin. He still couldn't believe it had worked. The gate had radiated such freezing cold when he approached, but the key had sucked the cold into itself, and for only an instant did it burn him like death, until the gate swung open and he could pass through. Then it all faded and the warmth of the sun returned.

Now he was in the queen's inner realm. He could see her castle ahead though it was shrouded in a kind of heat-like mist, as if the rays of the sun were bent and refracted to make a shield around her walls. He did not see the unicorn horn as it flashed, but he heard a raven cry and take off out of the corner of his eye. The only thing that saved him was Thorn's skin.

When the horn slashed, it cut through the guise of the wood grue, splitting the form in two. Tom rolled out like a pale stone, and whatever had wielded the horn took no notice. Off Tom ran, too shocked to look back or comprehend, fleeing as one hunted. The hide of the wood grue remained behind, a trophy for the hunter.

Tom ran to the swelling growth of trees to the east, an old forest of pine and aspen. His eyes were blurred with tears and terror, his feet barely feeling the pine needles and cones on the ground. He sped through the trees, huffing and gasping for breath. No looking back. No idea where to go.

He tumbled. A root caught his foot, or a stone. He

rolled into a heap, and when he opened his eyes, the towering spruce waved above him in the breeze. The sunlight filtered through like gossamer. Without thinking, his hand went to the key in his pocket. The throbbing cold was still there.

Something else cold was nearby. Something huge. Tom's gut clenched again. He didn't know what might be waiting here in the queen's deepest realm. He gripped the key inside his pocket as if it might help him stave off an attack. It was a desperate and silly hope. Still, he let the cold iron sting his palm.

He turned. A huge, pulsing heap rested behind him not five yards away. It was the color of coral but flecks of grey speckled it like shale dust. At first, Tom thought it was only a massive stone, but it breathed—slowly, in and out, a steady but slow rhythm—and then Tom caught sight of its head. Equine. Mane the color of sea foam. A pale golden disk was emblazoned above its eyes.

"Gallien?" Tom whispered.

The unicorn's voice rasped into the silent forest. "She..."

Tom rushed to him. "Don't speak! Save your strength!"

"Must..." The unicorn's eyes were wild with fear. "Cursed us..."

Tom didn't understand, but when he knelt at Gallien's head, he saw what the pale golden disk was: the last remnants of the unicorn's horn. It was shorn almost to the skin.

"The queen?" Tom asked.

But Gallien could only manage to exhale a rattled cough.

Tom didn't stop to think. He reached under the

massive creature and tried to lift him. It was impossible, but still, he tried. "You must stand, Gallien. You'll die if you don't!"

Gallien groaned as his eyes rolled back into his head.

Tom cried out and for a fleeting moment, Gallien's eyes fluttered open, wide and terrible. With a final gasp, he said, "The blood sword. Make it. Break the…"

Tom felt the body go rigid. He pulled his hands away as the dead flesh sunk to the ground. For a moment, Gallien's body looked like a statue, a sad monument to a noble lord. But then the moment was gone, the sun hid behind the clouds and trees, and Tom watched as Gallien's body began to decay almost instantly. Moss covered the flesh and bones, then fungi and dark soil, then, at last, a thousand tiny flowers the color of sea foam. Nothing was left of the unicorn but brown earth and those delicate white petals.

Tom could hardly believe it. He clenched his eyes shut, but still, the hot tears streamed down his cheeks. He had forgotten everything— the iron key, the queen, Gwen, his curse—and thought only of his sadness that someone so wondrous as Gallien the unicorn could be gone.

It was a long time before he opened his eyes. They blazed with anger. He knew who had killed this creature. He turned back toward the direction of the queen's castle. So much ruin and pain had come about because of this queen and her old ones and her desire for humans. Tom could not let it stand. He hardly remembered Gallien's last words, but he barely thought about anything other than stopping the queen, and vengeance.

Running as fast as he could, Tom let his anger carry him. He did not see nor have the faintest notion that above him, from out of the day-sky, a rain of stars fell from the heavens and landed on earth.

❧

"What do they call you?" This time the man asked the question.

The queen's lips curled up in a rueful smile. "I am the queen. That is what the world calls me."

"Have you no name?"

"Would you believe me if I said I don't remember?"

The man laughed. "Forgetfulness is catching."

The queen tried to laugh with him, but something tugged at her heart. His face was a mixture of mirth and pain, and every second they spent together made his eyes grow more and more distant. Soon, she feared, he would be as cold as the silver goblet on the table. Something was seeping out of him like water spilling through the floorboards. Forgetfulness *was* catching, but it was not by accident. The queen would not let herself feel guilty, but it was hard.

"What sort of kingdom is this?" the man continued. "Somewhere in my dreams, I remember a different realm, a place so familiar and yet so far from me. I can almost see it and then it's gone. The memories are like shadows."

The queen nodded. "I know such shadows. They follow me too, and when I try to make sense of them..."

Both were quiet for a long time. They looked out the window at the afternoon sky, the sun now past its noonday zenith and slowly tilting into the west. For a moment, the queen thought she saw something fall from the sky: a pale prick of light like a speck of dust, then another and another. But she shook her head and turned back to the man.

"I will give you a name," she said. "Let those old memories die in their shadows and face the new light of day with me." She stood up. "I will name you consort." She took his hand and held it to her lips.

He bowed his head. "My lady." Then he kissed her pale hand.

When he looked up, his eyes were even more distant. The warmth was almost drained. The queen suppressed her thoughts. She told herself she didn't need his heart, only let herself brush that lock of hair from his forehead and hold him near.

"My kingdom is called Illvelion," the queen began. She had to tell him some part of her story, to make him understand her desires, her confusion. He felt like the only person she could tell these things to.

"I do not remember when I came here," she continued, "and the tale of how I claimed the throne is too terrible to recount. But I was not always from this place. I was from some other place, some distant place, some realm that lay beyond the forest. I can see it when I close my eyes or when I hear a song sung in the night. It is often a man's voice who is singing."

She expected him to say something, but he was silent.

"And then, one day in that other place," she said more bitterly than she intended, "I fell."

The queen stopped. The words died on her lips and she didn't know why. All her shadowed memories vanished like wisps of smoke. The man said nothing but looked at her intently. "That is all," she said at last. "I fell."

"I hope you weren't hurt." The man's face was gentle, but his voice was hollow.

"I did not let it stop me. After a long struggle, I became queen." If she could not tell her story, at least she could wear her crown.

"Impressive."

"But I have always been alone." She betrayed not a hint of self-pity.

"No suitors?"

The queen shook her head and almost laughed. "None that suited me. Though I tried to make them."

"What makes me special?" He tried to smile again, but it was cold.

The queen took her fingers and brushed the unruly strands of hair from his forehead. "You remind me of someone."

"From that other place?" When the queen did not answer, he tried again. "And I did you a small service." The man looked at the unicorn horn resting on the queen's bed. "That must count for something."

His words shattered the moment. The queen scowled at the horn. Now she had to think again about the raven's report of a wood grue collapsing and a strange boy running into the ancient woods. When the man carried the wood grue back, her aged magisters had studied the body and told her it was just a skin, dead for many hours. And the strange boy, the raven had said, had looked *human*.

Bliss was turned bitter again. A human child.

What could it mean? Thoughts of the old ones prickled her skin like icicles.

"I demand a greater service," she said, at last, standing over him. "My enemies are within my gates and must be destroyed. Do not be fooled by appearances. The one who looks like a child is a servant to those who would crush me. Take up the horn again and slay him."

"A child?" Even though his eyes were cold and empty, something in him recoiled.

"An enemy." She picked up the horn and handed it to her consort. "My kingdom will die if he should live. All that I have made with my own hands will perish. We shall perish. Do not let it happen. Let us keep ourselves alive. I would not lose you so soon after finding you." She lifted her face toward his and dared something she didn't think possible. She kissed him and for the briefest of moments, she saw behind his face the face of another: blue eyes and tufts of golden hair upon a child's head. Then the face was gone and the queen realized her consort was returning her kiss, but it was the kiss of a stranger, cold and stiff and empty.

He took the horn again and bowed to her, and the queen rued the magic she had wrought.

❧

The queen's castle rested on a hill high above the glade where the iron gates stood. The hill itself was studded with huge stones, while an obsidian path circled its way through the stones to the peak. The castle was all stone too, alternating between basalt and quartz to make a black-and-white checkered pattern, like a chessboard in three dimensions. Four turrets bloomed around the castle's perimeter in a haphazard fashion, and atop it was a roof of thatched raven feathers. The doors to the castle were not doors at all but a heavy swirl of white mist which hovered inside a stone archway.

Tom ran for the castle with no plan and no thought of what he would do when he reached that misty doorway. All he thought of was Gallien's moldered body and Gwen and the hatred he had for the queen. Perhaps it was hatred for himself, for his part in Gwen's undoing, but that hatred was strong enough to carry him over the ground like a storm wind.

"Hold!" The queen's consort had appeared suddenly at the bottom of the stony hill. He held aloft a sword-like weapon, glimmering like burnished gold. When Tom saw what it was, his knees buckled. It looked ugly in the hands of this man who had no right to it. *This man...*

Something in the man's face was familiar. Tom found himself stumbling and trying not to fall. That face. It was like and yet unlike the face of one he knew.

"Come without struggle and you may plead the queen's mercy," the man said, still holding the horn as a threat.

Tom wished desperately that this faerie knight would spout blood and die just like all the others the queen had made. But he seemed hale and strong and shivered with a vitality that all those other false creations did not.

"Never!" Tom cried. "I defy her! You have no right to that sword!" Tom wasn't thinking. Fury clouded his wits. He reached into his pocket and pulled out the iron key, holding it high like a torch.

"Please," the consort said, pain in his eyes. He still had some sliver of heart left that made him ache to see this child so defiant and wounded, so brave. "Please come with me. I will—" The words clung to his lips. "I will protect you."

Tom laughed wickedly. "You'll fall to dust and flowers like all the rest. Nothing she makes ever lasts."

He felt triumphant in his angry taunts, and he didn't see as the raven swooped down out of the sky. The iron key was plucked from his grasp. All at once, his body felt lighter; the cold sting was gone. But his heart disintegrated in horror as he realized the key was gone. The raven could barely carry it in its beak —it burned too much—but its wings were swift and soon it had cleared the high walls of the castle, soon it would bring the key to the queen.

Tom's knees gave out. Crushed and defeated, he knew this was the end. He waited for the horn of the unicorn to slay him.

"Up, child, up!" called the consort. He was reaching down to Tom, extending a hand. "You are not a threat. Once the queen sees you, she will revoke her doom."

Tom crumpled like a brittle leaf. He didn't fight as the man lifted him and carried him up the hill. He didn't even see as they passed through the mists and entered the queen's castle. He had lost. Somehow he knew, with the key gone, with nothing to protect him, he was done for. There was no use in trying. He was at the queen's mercy now, and everyone knew, the queen had no mercy.

THE NEVER-ENDING MELODY OF NIGHT'S ENCHANTMENT

Her feet were covered in dirt so thick that Gwen thought she saw tiny mushrooms sprouting between her toes.

"Pay attention, not to feet or grime but to the wind." The red voice was somewhere above her, but she couldn't see where.

"Pay attention to the roots of trees," said the dark voice. It came from the depths of the earth where the thickest roots grow.

"And the stars," said the last voice, close to Gwen's heart. She couldn't see the last fairy either—all three were hidden from her—but she could feel the rapid beating of its heart. It was like the tumultuous beating of hummingbird wings.

There were no stars that she could see. It was before dawn, and the sky was at its darkest. To Gwen's eyes, it looked as if the stars had been blown out. There was no wind either. The calmness of the forest was frightening. Nothing stirred. No sound, no breath. All still. Only the voices of the three fairies surrounding her like smoke from a dragon's mouth.

"Pay attention," they all said at once. "Pay attention. Someone is coming."

Gwen didn't want to follow their commands. She wanted to stare at her dirty feet and go back to who she was before. She remembered her old self faintly, like a reflection in a pool of water. She had lived elsewhere, not in this forest, and she had danced in cool grass amongst the fireflies and stars. She had been a daughter, but to whom, she couldn't quite recall. He had a face that smiled and carved lines into his cheeks when he laughed. She wanted to go back to that place, beyond the forest.

"Remember our bargain," the last fairy said, then she saw it, its frog-like eyes glowing in her lap like two moonstones. The fairy held up the ball of clay and grinned. "Blood and stone and you know what to do," it said then slithered away into darkness.

Gwen wasn't sure how, but she knew suddenly that she was alone. The three fairies had gone. The sky was as black as ever, but now the forest lurched and stirred, and Gwen felt the ground beneath her rumble. Pebbles rolled away from her toward the western horizon. The ground underfoot, which was already moist with early morning dew, grew wetter and wetter until the soil was changed to mud.

Gwen stood up and looked around, straining her eyes to go deeper into the darkness. The earth shook again, and a huge smudge appeared in front of the trees before her. The smudge grew bigger as it moved closer, and the outline of its shape showed two thick legs supporting a barrel-like body and a head like a craggy boulder.

Gwen backed away from the horrible smudge, fear seizing her. She wanted the fairies to come back, to save her. But she was alone, and the monstrosity that looked like a vat of oil brought to life advanced upon her, shaking the ground as it stalked.

"Breaker of empires!" the thing cried, its voice thick with sludge. "Accursed human!"

Gwen had never seen the Mud Lord before, and yet she knew somehow that this was the creature who had built that vast empire upon the backs of slaves. She remembered how her fury broke those towers and ravaged that kingdom. She also remembered, faintly, how she lost control.

But that memory was a wisp of gossamer now, carried away by the slightest breath from Gwen's lips. Her fear went with it. What had she to fear from these threats? Hadn't she once opened a chasm in the earth to swallow up this creature's monstrosities?

She knew what to do. The eyes and the waiting breath of the three fairies were all around her, the thin fingers of the last fairy holding her blood in a ball of clay, and Gwen had barely to wish it when the earth split in two. The Mud Lord stumbled, his sludge spilling over the sides of the fissure, his feet dancing perilously close to the edge.

But he would not be deterred. He too had command of clay and earth, and with a bellow like a thunderclap, he poured his wrath into the fissure so that it ran wet with red mud. He was master of the element; he was vengeance. Soon he would bury this child in a grave as cold as stone.

Gwen remembered she was human now. She fell back, stuck her bare feet into the encroaching sludge, felt everything around her sinking. The trees, the sky, the clouds, all was sinking. There was no Gallien to save her now.

"Pay attention," whispered the red fairy. "Not to feet or grime but to the wind."

"Pay attention," they all whispered.

There was no wind. The air was heavy, choked by so much mud and hate. The Mud Lord was almost upon her, grinning madly, ready to make her his cornerstone, his foundation for a new empire.

"Pay attention."

Somehow, somewhere, Gwen heard a song.

The night extended for a little while longer; the sun refused to rise. And somewhere, in the night sky, Gwen heard a song as soft as the first tongue of the west wind on the first day of autumn.

She caught the melody and hummed it, thinking it the silliest thing she would ever do, to hum a tune while death was at her doorstep.

She hummed as the night sang, and the wind became a scythe, cutting across the earth like tempered steel. It was a death-blade, razor sharp and swift.

The grin of the Mud Lord was split in twain. The wind had sliced right through him. Another fissure in the earth.

His face fell sideways, severed from the neck, and the rest of him fell like a wet sack, spluttering as it landed on the forest floor.

The Mud Lord was no more.

Gwen heard the wind echo before it fled back to the heavens. Her humming voice dried up in her throat.

She could hardly think. Sinking to the ground, she pulled her knees tight against her chest.

Who was she? What had she become?

Seeing the Mud Lord cut in two was worse than

watching his kingdom be destroyed. She felt revulsion, but what frightened her, even more, was the way the revulsion seeped out of her and dissipated into the darkness.

A moment later, it was gone. Nothingness remained. She stared at the dead Mud Lord as if he were little more than a fallen tree limb.

She stood up and brushed off some flecks of red clay.

"What song was that?" she heard herself asking. Her voice was flat and passionless. "And how might I call it again?"

"Indeed, indeed," came the rasping whispers of the fairies. "We have hoped for this."

Now they came out of the shadows, and as they did, the first faint rays of sunlight crested the eastern horizon.

"The night has gone," Gwen said to herself.

The fairies circled her. "Not gone. Waits behind the sun-sky, and waits and waits."

"For me?" Gwen felt something stir inside. She liked the thought of calling back the night.

"Indeed," said the red fairy, holding the ball of clay aloft. "Strike a deeper bargain. With the night."

"With the song," added the dark fairy.

"With us," the last fairy finished.

Gwen knew, somewhere in the corridors of her heart, that a further bargain with these creatures was wrong, but she still tasted the hum of that night song in her throat, and she wanted more of it. The picture of the Mud Lord being killed had utterly faded from her mind; all she thought of was the power of the wind and the melody of the song.

"What must I do?" she asked.

The fairies circled closer. They came right up to her legs and the hem of her faded dress, and as they pressed closer, they passed the ball of clay between themselves, like children playing a game.

Gwen closed her eyes. She didn't want to see where they would cut her. A voice was crying out in her head, but it was muffled as if underwater. "Stop! No!" it cried, but Gwen overpowered it with the melody of the song. She pushed the song through her head, threading it all around like a string, tightening it in knots that could never be undone.

"Just like the other one," she heard the last fairy say, its voice muffled too. "She is doing it herself."

"Aye," said the other two. "She has struck the bargain."

"Unbreakable," the last fairy replied.

"Aye, aye," they answered.

No cut had been made; no blood spilled. The girl opened her eyes as if startled out of a dream. The fairies were out of sight.

I am alone at last, she thought. A smile crept across her lips. If anyone had chanced to walk by that part of the forest and glimpsed the girl, they would have seen a young woman with hair turned white and eyes as pale as pearls, and a dress that shimmered white like a star. As cold as those distant suns, she was like a pillar of white flame. None who knew her before would have recognized her. She stood straight and tall as a queen.

The fairies still watched her, their presence hidden by the trees and the spiders' webs and the dried leaves and the roots which crept across the forest floor. They watched and waited for her to call forth a song and show her power. They let her think she was alone, just as they had done those many years ago for another young woman in the forest, another enchantress.

The white-haired girl looked up to the sky, to the rising dawn. It was still early-morning pale, the sun still low in the east, and the stars faintly shone like pinpricks in the heavens. The girl hungered for those stars.

"Call them down," said no one but the roots of the trees. The girl heard the voice and obeyed.

From deep within her chest, where emptiness reigned, she called forth a song. It rose out of her throat and through her lips—a wordless song—and as she sang, the heavens shivered.

"Come!" she said through her song, though she spoke no words. "Come to me!"

The stars vibrated like tuning forks struck against iron.

"Come!" she said again, her song building to a crescendo.

It went on and on, past the dawn and into the morning, and at last, the song reached through the afternoon, and the stars vibrated but did not fall.

"Come!" she cried one last time, every note of the wordless song echoing her command. Her throat was raw from the singing, the emptiness inside her chest full to bursting.

She sang the final note.

From out of its crook in the sky, one tiny star fell. Then another. Then another and a dozen more, and still more fell, until a hundred stars had fallen and blazed around her like pools of white fire. They were as white-hot as she, their light extinguishing all else in view.

From their hiding places, the three fairies shielded their eyes and cowered a little. Even the sorceress they had made all those years ago could not bring down the stars.

But the child was not finished. As the stars burned around her like November haycocks, she called forth another song. This one stretched the stars and refashioned them, molding their forms into something almost human, until at last, they were human, in form if not in fact. Head and limbs and white-hot hearts that burned beneath the translucent skin, giving them a glow like fireflies. They were fireworks waiting to explode, but the enchantress modulated her voice and softly quelled their deepest fire, until the only light that burned came from around their eyes, a faint gleam that hinted at their celestial origins.

Then she sang a song like the crackling of a forge, and their bodies were swathed in glimmering armor, and swords and spears bloomed from their fingers, and all of them were arrayed as an army for their queen.

One hundred knights stood around her, with hair of flaxen gold, and boyish faces that smiled upon her, loyal and true.

The three fairies were now truly afraid. This was more than the old queen had ever made; her faerie knights had never been so many all at once. And these were not men of earth or even bone, but men made of star fire and cold night.

The young enchantress turned suddenly from her creations and searched for the three fairies. Even as she felt such power and emptiness that nothing could touch her, there were still moments when she felt lost, when she worried and yearned for someone to help her.

"What have I done?" she cried.

The fairies took their chance. They showed themselves once more and came close to the young one. The red fairy held itself wrapped in its wings. The dark fairy was little more than a shadow.

But the last fairy did not cower; it stood at the child's side and grinned. "You have made an army."

For a brief moment, the girl felt regret, but it dried up like a single drop of rain, and all she was left with was that thrilling emptiness.

"Yes," she said, savoring it. "An army."

"Now you must regain what you have lost," said the last fairy.

"Aye!" cried the other two fairies. "What you have been searching for!"

"Searching for?" replied the enchantress.

"Indeed. The queen and her iron gates. The one you seek. All shall be yours," answered the last fairy, licking its lips.

"The one I seek?" The young enchantress wasn't sure. Did she seek anyone? Who was there to seek, after all, when she could make figures out of starlight?

"Go!" the red and dark fairy cried. "To the iron gates!"

The iron gates meant nothing to the enchantress. The fairies seemed eager, but she felt empty. What was there to feel? she wondered. All that mattered was the power to call down the stars. All that mattered was the song that echoed the wind. The enchantress had these things, why did she need any other?

"Iron," she said softly. "There is danger in iron."

The last fairy nodded. "True. But their swords can break it." He pointed a sharp fingernail at the swords of the knights.

"And why should I want to break these gates?"

The fairies sucked in their breath and murmured. They rubbed their hands and claws and shadowed palms together, conspirators all.

"For a kingdom," said the red fairy.

"For a crown," said the dark fairy.

"For the one you seek," said the last fairy.

The enchantress glared at them. "I don't seek anyone. I never have and I never will." She looked at her army of gleaming knights, all of them as still as ice in deepest winter. She had what she needed, if she needed anything. And perhaps she needed nothing at all. That stirred the emptiness to a kind of ecstasy.

"Then for the crown," replied the last fairy, its voice weaker than before.

"Aye, the crown!" said the other two.

The enchantress had never considered a crown before. Perhaps in some earlier life, she had known of such things, but that earlier life was gone now, blotted out like salted earth, like a new moon in the empty sky. All that was and is and would remain was the empty song captured in her empty heart.

"Do I want a crown?" she asked herself and no one.

The fairies encouraged her, sounding almost desperate. It was a shock to them that their young ward would not want such power. Like a chorus, they advised her: "Take the crown, take the kingdom, break the gates, and rule!"

The enchantress shook her head. "None of that matters."

The last fairy felt its power faltering. "Then go for only one thing."

"One thing?"

"One thing only."

Neither the fairy nor the enchantress said a word. All the words died on the summer wind. The sun hung above in the afternoon sky, and the star-fire knights quivered as they stood on the forest floor. The enchantress watched them standing there, waiting for her command.

"One thing only," she said to herself, and with those words began to weave another song.

The army roused their stiffened legs and marched, swords and spears burning with white fire. The three fairies disappeared into the underbrush, following along, spurred by desire.

And the enchantress walked behind, her melody a rich and dark one, like the heavy air of an August midnight. She sang all the hollowness that was within her, all the heart and feeling that was missing, all the savoring of nothing that made her relish what she had become.

As she walked, she left the child behind—the child who had crossed the edge of the forest, who had come seeking her father, who had wreathed her heart with spells. She carried only herself, a pale figure humming the wind. And with every note, her emptiness grew, and the army of starlight swelled.

Once the footsteps of the army died away, the wild ones crept out of the brambles. They tilted their necks at the man who was left behind. He stood there gazing at an empty spot, a foot-trampled spot that was now a puzzle. Where had they all gone? And why didn't he go with them? He couldn't say. After all, he had no words yet.

The wild ones watched him for a span, then ventured forth. They knew the look he had; soon he would bleed and be gone, perhaps a mound of grass or moss upon a stone. One of the queen's faerie men.

But this one had a look that was not of the usual sort. The dog-headed jackdaw and the long-faced puck and the other wild ones started to see that this one was different. It bled with star fire. Its heart was cold heat. There would be no mound to commemorate him.

The wild ones watched as the man stared dumbly at the empty forest. He only glanced at them for a moment—a surprising moment, to see these creatures who lived in the world with him, whom he did not know until now, and whom he would never really know, not now or ever, as the fire and dust flamed out into the air—but at that moment, his eyes met theirs, and light wept out of him, and the wild ones were sad too.

This one was different. If only he could have stayed so.

But these things end. They always end. There is no changing the nature of things.

The starlight spilled out of his mouth and his fingernail, and soon all of him was weeping until he was a burst of light, a tiny star walking upon the earth.

The wild ones backed away, fearful. The man tried to follow them, but his steps were hollow. In a flare of light that washed out the color of everything around him, the man melted into a pool of quicksilver, like the tears of a cobalt dragon. The wild ones stayed hidden, and when their eyes could see again, when the light flare effect had dissipated, they looked at the spot where the man had been and saw nothing.

Shrugging and sighing, they moved on. Like snails, they crept deeper into the forest to find something to fill their bellies, for they were hungry and couldn't be fed on the memory of starlight. They left that sad memory behind, hoping to forget.

THE IRON KEY

The queen sat alone in the highest tower of her castle. Twilight had almost arrived. She barely looked at the key in her hand; instead, her gaze went out the window. Somewhere out there in the gathering gloom of the forest was the one who would destroy her. She knew it now. The little puck had boasted as much. He had spoken nonsense, of course. Things about vengeance and the unicorn and something called a blood sword, and a girl. But underneath all of his ravings were true prophecies. She could feel it. She had been feeling it for a long time.

There was another. Younger, more powerful. A rival to march through the gates and supplant her. She knew it was not long now. She could feel it.

The trees swayed as if in answer to her worries. Now that she had finally found a consort worthy of her affections, it would all come crumbling down. Like dried clay turned to powdered dust. The wind would knock down her kingdom as surely as a hollow tree, rotten from too much age and too many rough storms.

Though she would not look at it, the queen knew what the key meant. She knew that it came from the same source as the iron of her gates. And whoever had called forth the iron of this key had the power to destroy the iron gates themselves.

She squeezed her fingers around the cold iron and let it sting her skin. It was faint—not nearly as painful as what the creatures of this forest would feel —but it was enough to remind her that she too was of the forest now, a creature of faerie as well. She had always tried to deny it, to remember herself as a human, but that was a lie. Her heart did not beat like a human's; her blood did not run hot through her veins. She was something else altogether, neither human nor fairy. Her playacting was at an end.

"My lady." The consort spoke to her through the heavy door. "You mustn't."

What did he think would happen? she wondered. Did he really think they could win this fight? He was a gallant fool. She had destroyed his humanity with a spell, and now he thought he could save hers with his courage. A sword and a fighting spirit. That was all her consort knew of fending off disaster. But that would not do. Not this time.

The queen laid the key down on the window sill. She studied it, tracing its curves and intertwined filigree with her eyes. It matched the ornament on her gates. Whoever made it was familiar with her spells, with the twisting of her desires.

Gallien.

Hadn't he helped her fashion the gate to keep the old ones out, to free her from their thrall?

If the queen could have sorrowed, she would have sorrowed for the unicorn. Not because she knew her doom was near and he might have saved her. Not even because she had killed him and was sorry. She almost sorrowed for him because once he had helped her. Because once she had asked for help.

Standing, she walked across the small room and ran her fingers over the interlocking stones of the wall. Feeling for the spot, she found a place where the mason had left some gap between the stones, and prying with her fingers, she moved one small stone from its place.

In the open crevice, a small willow wood box was hidden, polished smooth and unadorned. She took it out and opened it. There it was: her ring. She couldn't remember when she had taken it off, but she knew it was from her other life. It held great power, but she was always afraid to use it. Like herself, it had been transformed when she had crossed the edge into Illvelion.

"A ring of dreaming," she whispered. She slipped it on her finger and felt tears well in her eyes. If she wasn't careful, a flood would break. She swallowed the flood and hardened herself. If she were to die, at least she would be wearing this ring. As silent as owl wings, she put the box back behind the stone and all was as before.

The queen's heart was now storm-hale. She couldn't ask her consort for help, and she couldn't ask her subjects. They were like her: pawns and cold things. There was no one who cared, not truly. The iron key could not open any of them, nor herself. Only the gates, which she had made, and even those would now be set upon by someone mightier and more terrible. Soon they would break.

"My lady," the consort said again, a simulacrum

of tenderness in his voice. He feigned concern very well.

"Go," she replied. "For a little while. Let me think." Such lies they spoke to one another.

She heard his footsteps shuffle along the corridor. She was relieved to hear him go, but then without thinking or even knowing why she called him back.

"Bring me the puck," she said.

She didn't have a plan, but something about the key made her recall the puck's words from earlier, when he had been dropped at her feet, a prisoner. At first, all he had done was stare glassy-eyed at her face, seeing right through her into nothing. But when she had taken out the key and held it before him, when she had questioned him about it, suddenly fire had come into his eyes, and fury. Life had filled his breath, and he raged.

"You'll be destroyed, just you wait!" the puck had cried. "Gallien cursed you, and Gwen will find a way. I believe in her. She'll find a way to escape. And we'll make the blood sword and destroy you!"

At the time, the queen took little notice of these ravings. Gallien was dead. And a human child could not find her way within the forest. And the blood sword? The queen had never heard of a blood sword.

But the words suddenly clawed at her, scratching an itch in her mind. The puck had said *make*. Make the blood sword.

He was as defiant as ever when they brought him again to her high tower.

"That key doesn't belong to you," he spat. "You're a thief!"

The queen didn't reply. She looked at him intently, studying his face. "Why do you appear human?" she said. "You claim to be a puck, but I see no trace of that kind in you."

He wouldn't answer. His mouth was as thin as the blade of a knife.

"I can get the answers from your dreams," the queen said, raising her left hand slightly. The sapphire ring glinted. "My ring can make you dream, and in your dreams, you can tell me whatever I want."

"Try it then," the puck answered. "If your magic be powerful enough." He did his best to sneer at her. "See what my dreams tell you."

The queen kept her temper. "Perhaps I shall. Though you are right to guess that my magic is weakened. If you are a puck, then your transformation to human is flawless. Only the most powerful spell can do such as this."

"Cursed, you mean," replied the puck. "Cursed I am to be like you."

The queen laughed a cold and merciless laugh. "You mistake me. I am not human. Not anymore. A most powerful spell has cursed me too." Her laugh died away, and a deep sadness overtook her face. She looked at the human-like creature with tenderness. "Who cursed you, little puck?"

He couldn't remember. He groped for the memory, scavenging like a hungry rat, but the time before he was human was as dark as a starless night. He realized suddenly that he had always assumed it was Thorn who had cursed him, but that couldn't have been. He was human when Thorn found him. Always human, as long as he could remember.

"I suppose you hope I'm a real human," he said.

"Then you can drink my blood and keep yourself forever young."

This time the queen didn't laugh. She could hardly make a sound. The accusation was as horrible as the idea itself. Drinking blood didn't keep oneself young. *How in the world did this puck come to such an idea?* The thought horrified her.

The revulsion in the queen's face must have changed something about her features—softened them or made them sad—for the puck looked at her suddenly as if he knew her, as if he had seen both a friend and a ghost.

"You—" he started but never finished. Then he looked wildly around the room as if he expected someone else to appear. "Where is your faerie knight?" he said. "Has he died yet and turned to flowers?"

The queen recovered herself. "Not this one," she said. "Never this one. He is my consort now and forever until my doom comes."

"Never?" The puck's face had turned as white as the full moon. He looked the queen full in the face. He recognized that face. "You don't know who you are, do you?"

The queen touched her forehead and the sapphire stone in her ring seemed as huge as the sky. "This forest makes us all forget. You should know that, little puck who was never a puck."

"I was!" But he wasn't so sure.

"And I was a human, but all of that is lost now."

"It's not! You say you don't know Gwen, but I think you do, and when you see her you'll understand. Maybe even you'll remember. She's been looking for you, though she doesn't know it. And your faerie knight too. You were human once, just as she!"

"You're talking nonsense again, and I grow weary." She sat down in the seat by the window and looked out the shimmering pane of glass. "Perhaps I will make us all dream. Cast us into sleep and shroud the castle in a deep fog. My rival will never find us then."

Tom didn't like the sound of this. "Just disappear? Is that your answer to everything?"

"What else can I do? Unless you know another way." The queen picked up the iron key almost without thinking, but she could feel the puck's eyes on it. "I have wondered about your words. About the blood sword." She didn't know why, but her voice quivered when she said it.

Now the puck looked chastened. His head drooped again. "A bluff. I don't know what it is nor how to get it."

"But you said *make*. Make the blood sword."

"Did I? Well, that was Gallien's talk. He said it would break—" He looked up. "The curse. That's what he meant. It would break the curse."

The queen felt the key begin to burn her palm. She did not let it go. "How do we make the blood sword?" Her eyes were gathering tears, for she seemed to know even as Tom did that they were close to unraveling something.

"I don't know," said Tom. "I wish I did. Gallien didn't say."

The key was as hot as an ember in the queen's hand. She had to drop it or it would brand her flesh. The little key clanged heavily on the stone floor. Both the queen and the puck stared at it for a long moment.

"Gallien made that," whispered Tom. "Out of the chain Gwen carried. Opens the gates, it does."

"The gates I made to keep all enemies out," the queen rejoined. She was lost in her thoughts, talking to the air. "I do not have a knife. Must it be my own? How long will it take, then? I fear we have lost the time." She began to pace the room, talking under her breath.

Tom wasn't sure what to make of the queen's words. She mumbled to herself, not to him. Her face had a slightly crazed look, and he could see the wizardry in her eyes. This was the queen who so many in the forest feared. But Tom was not afraid. Now that he understood, now that he knew her for what she really was, he didn't fear her.

The queen called out for her consort. He appeared without delay as if he'd been waiting just outside the door. The horn of Gallien was still in his hand, its sharp edge at the ready.

"My lady." He bowed low, and when he looked at the queen and then at the puck, Tom was sure of it all. These were faces he knew, reflections of another.

"Take your weapon and give me a wound," the queen said. "Not too grievous, but enough to draw blood."

The consort drew back. "Never! I cannot!"

Something in the way he said it made Tom think the consort was merely reciting lines, playacting as a noble servant but empty of real feeling. Still, the consort recoiled as the queen moved closer.

"You must," she said. "I command it. Or give me the horn and I shall do it myself." Tom thought she had never looked more fearsome nor more sorrowful.

The consort gave in. His feigned concern now

shifted to cold duty, and yet still, Tom wondered if he had any feeling at all or was simply acting the part.

"Here," said the queen, stepping back toward the key on the floor.

"Where shall I make the wound, my lady?" the consort asked. "Not too grievous, yet enough."

The queen thought a moment. Tom had shrunken back into the shadows of the room and watched the scene play out like a mummers' masque. He watched the queen consider where she would take her wound, and it was like watching her thoughts emerge like phantoms and circle around her like snakes. She considered her breast, just above the heart, and her wrist, the veins of life, and even her thigh, a crippling wound. But the queen had not the courage for those cuts, and instead held out her hand, the left hand where the sapphire ring glimmered.

The consort saw the glint of the jewel at the same moment he took the edge of the horn and ran it down the queen's pale skin. The jewel made him gasp, like a drowning man coming up for air, and he almost tried to stop the horn from splitting the queen's skin, as if he realized too late what he was doing.

Drops of heavy blood splattered down onto the stone floor, pooling themselves on top of the iron key and around it, and the queen clutched her hand in pain while more blood seeped between her finger, while the consort dropped the horn and stared disbelieving at the sapphire ring which now was stained red. All of this happened in a flash, and then the queen called out to her servants to come quickly, and while she called, the consort fled from the tower. The queen did not bandage her hand for she had nothing with which to do so, but Tom took off his cap and gave it to her, helped her wrap it around the wound, and suddenly a flurry of strange creatures were with them: the raven and a snake-headed fox and a stout pig who walked upright.

"Take the key," the queen said, her face pale. "As quick as you can, forge me a sword."

The creatures looked around, confused. "Not enough iron," the pig grunted, head bowed in contrition. "Begging pardon."

"It will serve," the queen said as the blood soaked through Tom's hat. "Do as I say."

The creatures said nothing more but took the bloody key and left.

"How long will it take?" the queen said to herself. She went back to the window and looked out, searching the darkness beneath the trees for some sign of her enemies. She fingered the sapphire ring as she held Tom's cap against her wound. "Perhaps," she said. "Perhaps."

Tom watched her in silence. The horn of Gallien rested on the floor, streaked with the queen's blood, but he would not look at it. If he did, he would weep.

"It may work," the queen said softly. "Perhaps."

It was the last thing Tom heard.

The consort saw the sapphire ring even now, even as he was alone on the staircase. It lingered in his mind like a bright flash of light lingers in one's sight even after the flare has gone. That sight stirred something deep inside. A horrible feeling, a terror-stricken feeling. It was a feeling of losing and finding and losing again all at once. He straddled a dream and a nightmare as he stood there alone, the door to the queen's tower looming above him. Something warm as blood started to fill his chest.

"Bronwyn," he said, the word sticking in his throat. "Gwen." He closed his eyes. The tears fell anyway.

He wanted to rush back into the room, to take the queen into his arms. He remembered her kiss, the one that had been so empty, and he tried to will its memory into something more.

It was useless. He was caught between tides: the memories filling his heart were only white feathers floating on the waves, all of them slowly receding out to sea, just beyond his reach. As those feathers floated away, something else came rushing in with greater force, something that submerged his true feelings. He stood like a man straddling a chasm, waiting as the world broke further and further apart.

He didn't even notice as the queen's servants came up the stairs and then moments later came back down, carrying the bloodied key reverently, like a glass scepter. He stood as still as glass himself, waiting as his memories drifted into the air. Into nothingness.

When he was empty again, he wondered if he should return to his queen, to beg her for some service, for something to show his devotion. His mind was devoid of any of those passions which had been with him only moments before. All he could comprehend was that he was her consort and she his queen. But something in the back of his mind told him this was all a spell, all a fantasy. He could not move. He could not decide. And as he stood waiting, hoping for something within to break open, he felt a deep and heavy sleepiness come upon his eyes. Mist and darkness veiled his sight. Like a child's rag toy dropped to the floor, he fell on the step and went still. He slept and went instantly into his dreams.

❧

Where the queen's castle had been, nothing remained but a heavy fog. The hill was shrouded in thick mist, and all the lands around it, and the ancient trees were lost in the whiteness of the cloud. All within the castle slept, all except the servant who manned the forge and the smith who wielded the hammer.

Deep within the under-bowels of the castle they worked, hot and sweaty with toil. The furnace was like a burning heart within the innermost cavity of the fortress, and the two creatures of the queen kept at their work, fanning the flames and striking the hot iron.

For the iron key was their work, and though it was small, it did not diminish. It grew with each hammering, it flourished under the heat. Both the smith and his prentice watched in awe, with sweat dripping down their leathery brows, as the iron key gave way. It took a long while, but slowly it stretched to a thin and perfect blade.

And as they worked, the world around them slept. And dreamed.

But the creatures at the forge did not dream. Instead, they worked and crafted, and at last, they had made the sword. The prentice—a slight skrit with a scorpion's tail—cooled the iron in a vat of water, and steam sprayed around them like a mist of rain. The smith, his pig-snout sniffing with satisfaction, took the weapon and appraised it. He had done little to shape it, only to hammer it, and somehow, through its own magic, the sword had formed. The pommel resembled still the form and filigree of the key's bow, and the end of the blade still had traces of the key's bit and wards, shaped as they were with three clefts. The clefts on the end of the blade were sharper now, ready for unlocking whatever soft flesh they met.

The smith grunted and he and the prentice made ready to offer their work to the queen. Long hours had passed, but they were unaware, and the dreaming castle above them was still a mystery. For what purpose had the queen wanted this blade, her servants did not know, but when they held it, they felt a fearsome magic, and terror ran through their thin blood. What, they wondered, had the queen wrought? And what now would she do?

"Gone!" cried the red voice.

"Vanished!" cried the dark voice.

But the last voice knew better. "Hidden. Veiled. The last of her powers."

"But how?" the red voice demanded.

None of the old ones knew. This magic was beyond their bargain with the queen.

"If it's hidden, we shall find it," said the enchantress. She stepped lightly to the edge of the clearing. Her pale eyes searched through the fog for some sign of her enemy's castle. "We have the starlight, do we not?" She gestured to her army, arrayed behind her like a thousand flecks of moonlight on the surface of a glassy pool. "She cannot hide forever."

The iron gates were not shrouded by fog. They stood like a row of iron guards, unmoved and unmoving, a warning to all who dared approach. The three fairies shrank from the bars of the gates, feeling their cold sting even from a distance. The queen's magic was weakened, but even still, there were times when the gates held fast.

"She has strengthened them," growled the dark one.

"It will not last," said the last. "Even now, they grow brittle."

The enchantress had no fear. She left the others behind and approached the gates, hand outstretched. She wasn't sure what to expect, but she knew she need not fear. These gates would have made her shiver in times past; their strangeness and their silence would have frightened her. But now, she considered them as nothing more than what they were: brittle bars of iron. They were gates, and gates were meant to be both closed and opened.

Lightly, her fingers brushed the cold metal. A sharp sting danced across her skin, but it felt strangely good. She hadn't felt something that keen in a long time. With one swift movement, she clutched the bars with both hands and let the cold bite her. The iron burned her flesh, and tears came to her eyes. She relished them. She hadn't felt the need to cry in a long time. Yet she was in control.

With all the force she could muster, she pushed the gates open on their ancient hinges. As she let go of the bars, the immediate pain of the cold iron dissipated, but the enchantress could remember the deep burning of the pain long afterward. It was the only thing she could remember.

"Come," she said to the air, but her army heard her. She walked through the gates and they followed. Even as she went, she knew that something must be done to heal the pain of the iron's bite. The mists swirling around the queen's hill slithered through the air like thin, wispy snakes. With a soft hum of her lips, the enchantress called the mists and they gathered around her like mounds of silk. Cold and damp, the fog wetted her burnt hands and healed them, and then it settled upon the army as they entered the gates, and the air around the starlight men glimmered with softened light.

The hill lay bare, uncovered from its misty blanket. Upon the black rocks stood the queen's abode, silent and grim. Nothing stirred within or without.

The enchantress laughed. It had been too easy. The old powers were fading, and soon her new strength would supplant these old ways. Behind her, the three fairies nodded and rubbed their clawed hands together, but they walked warily behind the young woman and her army. Her power was greater than the queen's, but so was her will, and the fairies worried that they had unleashed something they could not control.

CHAPTER ELEVEN
THE BLOOD SWORD

The grass was wet with dew, and twilight hung heavy over the meadow. The trees of the nearby forest were as dark as pitch. Not a single firefly lit the lawn. The musicians took out their fiddles and drums and penny flutes, but none said a word. The revelers all were quiet. No one breathed except the wolfhound by their lord's side. His shaggy, heaving breaths cut through the stillness like a forlorn ghost. All waited for the moon to shine brighter in the darkening sky. Then the dance would begin.

But the lady broke the silence. She laughed clear and strong, like a high-pitched bell in the churchyard. Everyone gasped. To break the silence before the first clap and drum was a taunt to the fairies. The moon was not ready.

And yet the lady laughed, and then her husband, their lord, laughed too, and at his signal, the music began. Revelers spun and jigged and danced with wild abandon, but none wilder than the lady herself, the woman clad in starlight white with a coronet of sapphires on her brow.

The dancers made a circle around her as she spun, and they clapped and howled like dogs at the twirling moon upon the lawn. Her lord watched from outside the circle, but then a reveler grabbed his hound and two other men pushed him into the circle, and soon he had clasped hands with his lady and danced.

He laughed heartily with her as they danced, and never once did he notice her eyes glance waywardly upon the woods. Too taken with her beauty and with the fury of the dance was he to notice the slight flit of her eyes in that dark direction.

The reel continued unto almost midnight, and then the revelers sighed and said, "Enough, the fairies should be satisfied now!" and all collapsed upon the moonlit grass with sweaty faces. The lord and his lady had regained their composure, and solemnly, with nary a word, they led their people away from the lawn and the edge of the forest and back up the hill to the manor house.

Tom watched them go. He hid amongst the tangle of brambles and thorns just on the other side of the woods. He felt somehow that he knew the lord and lady, but this was a dream, and in dreams, nothing is for certain. Their faces shifted in and out of focus, and it was more a feeling of knowing than of anything he could claim for true.

He watched them go and wondered why they had danced so. Was it for him? There were no other fairies in the forest with him. The woods were a black and blank space behind him, the edges of the dream world. Why should human dancing have satisfied anything at all? Perhaps it was more of the dream logic: the seeming of things but not the being.

Still, he remembered the lady's face, and her eyes

as they glanced evermore at the edge of the woods, and she seemed to be looking right at him, hungering for him or something past him in the darkness, even as she danced so happily with the lord. Tom wondered what her looking could mean.

The darkness came swiftly now, and soon it was deepest night when even the stars were hidden by clouds, and Tom knew this was a dream because time shifted, but no time went by, and suddenly there was a whiteness tripping over the grass, light as mist, and it was the lady. She had stolen away in the night. She crept to the edge of the forest. Like a wax candle glowing from within, she stole across the border between forest and lawn, pale as the moon. Tom was invisible to her; she passed right by him without a glance. Her eyes were fixed on something else, something deeper. Into the woods she went, a shadow in white.

A cry went up from the manor house early in the morning before the sky had turned pale yellow. A babe's cry. A wailing. There was no mother's embrace to comfort her.

"Our lady has died," they said. "In the night, she died."

All the folk around the land said the same sad whisper. The lady of Estline had died, and left her baby without a mother. Tears drowned the houses and the fields, and for long years, the lord never came again to the fairy lawn and the dance.

But Tom knew otherwise. He had seen her walking through the trees. Not dead, but gone. Chasing after something, hunger in her eyes.

He grew drowsy. All his vision became a haze of greens and yellows. The forest was erased by a drizzling fog. The last thing he heard was the cry of a baby, shrill and heartbroken.

❧

There was neither day nor night now. Everything was gray. But the queen's castle was clear as crystal resting on its hill of black obsidian. The enchantress marched her army up the hill to the open archway—for no swirling mist blocked it now—and entered. The three fairies followed, keeping their distance but waiting for the blood to flow. When it did, they would feast, and all of Illvelion might be theirs again. *Let the two destroy each other,* they hoped. *Let there be oblivion.*

❧

She had traveled far, despite the unicorn's warnings. *Would it even work?* she wondered. She watched her hand drift in and out of view and then change altogether into the seashore.

Her plan had changed now. No more bloodshed. Gallien had been right about that. She always took things too far. Pushed too hard. Wanted what she wanted and damned the consequences.

Not this time. Enough blood. Enough.

The wound on her hand was gone. She watched her fingers and then her palm return from the seashore. All around was sand and sea, nothing more. Would this work? She didn't know, but she had to try.

It had been a long time since she sang to the sea. The old ones had wanted fire or dark clumps of earth;

she had wanted the sea. Something fathomless had called to her.

Why am I doing this? she asked. *What was that sword for except to destroy my rival?*

And yet she was here, on the seashore, listening for a song. The song was the only thing that mattered. Hadn't it been that way long ago when she first came to the forest? She heard the song that night on the grass, a song only for her, and she followed it. It led to the sea.

She saw that she was dressed in peasant garb, a simple dress of hemp, almost the color of the sand beneath her feet. No longer a queen but simply a woman *Oh, to stay here and hide forever! To listen to the sea and hope for the song!*

But that dream—this dream—had always been an illusion. Hadn't her long years in Illvelion taught her that? The song did not fill her heart the first time; it would not fill her this time either.

But it might save him. It might. She had to try. Enough blood had been spilled.

She listened, hoping for the mournful cry, the quivering lilt. It would come from far off—just like the first time—and drift through her head like a thought. Then she would catch it up, join her voice to its far-off call, and together they would sing. Searching the sky, she hoped for some sight of it. The waves came in steadily, making a rhythm that reminded her of her own long-ago heartbeat.

But she had no heart to beat. She had given that up when she made her first bargain. Fear, then panic, then despair came crashing into the shore. What if it never came? What if all her deeds of these long years kept it away?

All of a sudden, the sea stood still. The waves stopped. Even the clouds hung frozen in the sky. And in her head, or across the waters, or somewhere beyond the dream, she heard it. She saw the white feather on the wing. She opened her mouth to call.

§

The queen stirred. Tom was already awake and by her side. The cut on her hand had begun to scab and crust over. Tom's hat clung to her palm, brittle with the flaking blood.

"There's noises," he said. "A rumbling of footsteps. Something's come inside your walls."

The consort rushed through the door looking pale. "My lady," he said, breathless, shutting the door behind him. "All your servants are gone. We are alone."

A sword hung above the door, its scabbard gilded and encrusted with jewels. He took it down and unsheathed it. The blade was still sharp.

The queen was unperturbed by her consort's haste. "Perhaps it is for the best," she said. She went to her bed and sat down. "I am weary."

"What's coming?" asked Tom. His head was still clouded. Everything felt as unreal as a dream.

"Where did the servants go?" asked the consort. "We are like living souls in the land of the dead."

The queen nodded. "Perhaps."

They all waited as a strange heat pulsed from the walls and door of the chamber. It was hot but cool, like the sting of iron.

"What comes?" asked the consort, fear creeping into his empty heart.

"Perhaps my new-forged weapon is ready," replied the queen. "But if the servants are all gone—"

She never finished her thought. Light as strong as the sun but pale as snow filtered in around the doorframe, filling the queen's high chamber with its brightness. Both Tom and the consort covered their eyes, but the queen did not flinch. She welcomed the blindness.

❧

"Hustle now!" cried the smith. "The light's coming!"

The prentice and the smith hurried from the bowels of the castle up to the queen's tower, but as they went—up crumbling dirt tunnels, through hidden passages buried in the walls, around and around spirals of weathered stone staircases—they could feel something pulsing behind the walls, something brighter than bright. It was like a sea of light came flooding over the castle faster than they could run, and the smith feared that soon the light would burst through the stone walls and drown them.

The prentice carried the sword, wrapped in a silken cloth, as if he were cradling a newborn human babe. This might be the last thing they would ever craft. He wasn't about to lose it to the coming storm.

"Quickly!" urged the smith. The light around them grew brighter; it seeped through the cracks in the walls. Soon they would be buried.

The prentice wondered if this last service would be good, if it would help the queen. Would she use the sword to stop the light?

The smith's cloven feet clicked furiously on the steps, the prentice's long toenails did the same, his

148

long tail waving behind him like a liquid trident. They ran till they were almost out of breath—heaving and puffing—and still, they ran.

But the way ahead was blocked. A man as bright as starlight stood there, burning the world down around them.

❧

"Where has she gone?" asked the red voice. "Cannot smell her."

"Too bright!" cried the dark voice.

"I hear the clang of blades," said the last voice, filled with dread.

❧

Steal did bite iron. The consort could not believe that he was still standing, but stand he did, sword flashing hot against the other man.

But he was not a man. He was a flame of white light, every part of him beaming with starlight. The only thing that the consort could truly see was the sword: thin black iron with three sharp clefts near the tip of its blade. The enemy wielded it against him with furious speed. The consort knew that soon the battle would be over. The other man was too strong, and the light blinded the consort's eyes.

But he couldn't abandon the queen. He would fight to his death if it could give her some small chance to escape. This was his part to play, his role to fulfill. Even as he fought with desperate savagery, he did not feel any fury or passion rising within. Only duty. Only his part. That feeling from earlier on the stairs had gone completely. He was merely the consort. The queen's own.

But even that duty could not sustain him. The starlight man was too swift, too quicksilver to parry, and the clefts found flesh. The consort felt his innards begin to spill out of the horrible thrice-deep gash. He lunged forward with his sword, but it was a paltry thrust. The star man paid no mind at all. Stepping lightly, he moved past the consort, careful not to slip on the other man's blood.

Sometime after he fell—moments only—Agravaine remembered. He remembered everything. His name, his quest, his love.

All the spells which had been twisted around his heart were released. All the emptiness was filled with something warm.

"My Gwen..." he gasped, voice choking on blood. Her face filled his vision. She stood looking down at him, imperiousness in her face. "My girl..."

But the young girl before his eyes moved past him, nary a glance at his dying form.

"My child..." Agravaine's eyes filled with darkness. The last thing he remembered was the hem of her dress, all the color gone, ripped and torn a little from his rough hands when he tried to save her, long ago, when she had fallen over the edge. He had not saved her. The fairies had their feast.

His final thoughts were of that moment. How long ago had it been? *How long... How long...*

The queen did not fight back. She smiled at the starlit warrior, his iron sword grim and dripping with her consort's blood.

"It shall do what it was made to do," she said, softly. "I should have foreseen."

The enchantress stood behind her warrior, looking pleased, but the queen caught her look and hurled it back. She would end without cowering. Without fear. Let this young usurper have her victory. But what she would never have was the queen's will.

"He is quite flawless," the queen said as the warrior raised his sword. "But I prefer my own."

The last thing she saw was her consort, his face strangely warm and peaceful even in death. Oh, how she longed to run her fingers through his hair! He looked more real—more himself—now than he had in life. The spell she had given him was gone.

The warrior's thrice-cleft blade cut the folds of the queen's dress, and with it, the wreath of her flesh was sundered. She cried out.

And remembered.

Everything, oh, everything! That night, the faerie reel, the hidden stars, the forest, the path to freedom. How foolish had she been! How young!

My child, my Gwen! What have I done?

⁊

"A feast."

"Aye, real blood."

"No more enchantments. True humans at last."

The old ones crept towards the man and woman lying on the stone floor. They would deal with the other one soon enough, but now it was time to feast.

No mere tinctures would they have; they would have all. First, the red one, groping with leathery wings. Then the dark one, barely a shape, merely a shadow. Then the last one of all, greed and gluttony in its fathomless eyes. This is what they had hungered for: the woman crowned as queen, bargainer turned thief, and her lover, a piece of her heart. This would satiate them—for a time—give them back some share of what they'd lost. Then their pawn would be next.

The enchantress saw them move, careful yet somehow swift, and with a word, she commanded her warriors to encircle the dead.

"No. You shall not have them." She stepped towards the starlight warrior who held the iron sword. "The look upon their faces. Did you see it? Before they died. What could it mean?" Her voice was strained, and suddenly she sounded more like the young girl she was than the enchanter of stars and wind she had become.

The three fairies bit their tongues. They let her play at having power. Just for a bit. They crept back from the circle of starlight.

The enchantress looked at her men as they crowded into the room, searching for answers in their blank, unthinking faces. She turned to the fairies.

"What did it mean? That look?" The coldness within tried to steel her voice, but it wavered.

She didn't see the boy cowering beneath the windowsill. She didn't watch him as he slinked along the floor toward the unheeded unicorn's horn, still crusted with the woman's blood. She didn't know he was near her until he spoke.

"You don't know what you've done. Those were your parents, true as blood." He held up the unicorn's horn. "And here's a thing too. Gallien's horn. Say you can remember! It's me, Tom!"

The words meant nothing to the enchantress. Her emptiness was renewed. She barely regarded the boy or his trinket.

"You have found what you seek," hissed the last fairy, a serpent at her feet. "That is what they were. And now you have it. The crown." He pointed a long fingernail between the feet of the warriors toward the queen's crown.

"Take it," said the red fairy.

"Have it," said the dark fairy.

"Yours to command," said the last fairy. "Illvelion."

Tom was crying. This was all his fault somehow, he was sure of it. If only he hadn't told Gwen a lie. If only he hadn't believed one about the queen.

The light spilling from the star men blazed like a sun, and Gallien's horn caught the light and flared. Tom was blinded, hot tears stinging his face. Everything in his vision was spotty and too bright, but the three fairies shimmered in his view, creeping toward Gwen, or himself. He couldn't be sure. They looked like demons.

Somehow the horn of Gallien slashed through the air toward the three. An arch of iron swung down on him, and Tom felt hot and weak, almost feverish. He heard a clang and realized he'd dropped the horn. His hands tried to catch his fall, and when he caught a glimpse of them, they were ruddy and hairy, like roots pulled up from the ground. He fell.

"I did not command you!" the enchantress cried, her wrath unleashed upon her starlit warrior.

The warrior looked dumbstruck. He had tried to

save his queen. Destroyed her attacker. Why did she look at him with such fury and grief? The iron sword hung limply in his hand, fresh with the boy's blood. He let it fall. The starlight within him spilled forth, and soon he was all light, an orb of heat, then a pool of quicksilver. Then gone.

The enchantress regarded the dead puck on the floor. She searched his face, with its root-like nose and crinkled skin, and wondered if this new face was an enchantment or if the other one had been. A thin crack shivered through her coldness. "I wish I could remember you."

The three old ones took their chance in the confusion. Enough niceties. The queen was dead. All were dead except the men of light, but even they were beginning to collapse. Now was the time. The gates would break, disorder again in Illvelion. The fairies ascendant.

The enchantress's army burst into pure light. One hundred supernovas. Brighter than suns. White and hot and blinding. Everything was starlight.

The enchantress closed her eyes, and the three fairies too, and all the castle disappeared in the brightness of that death.

From out of the white sky came an anguished cry. Flying over the ruins was a bird the color of sea foam. And with it came a wave from the far-off sea.

CHAPTER TWELVE

THE SEA FOAM BIRD

Gray sea, gray waves, gray tomb. Grayness and grayness, all around, grayness. Even the dark one could not blacken the gray. Even the red one could not brighten it. Even the last one could not hold it back. In their mouths, through their nostrils, into their ears, and all around, the water came, rushing and pounding and crashing, cold and salty and gray. Water deep and never-ending. Enough to drown the world.

Their only consolation was that the humans would die too. Vengeance at least.

All around, the stones of the castle floated in the depths. All around, the bars of the iron gates dropped like broken spears. All the detritus of Illvelion sank.

The last thing the old ones saw was the white wing of a bird or the glint of the far-off sun.

&

"You called me," the bird said.

"Yes."

"After all these years?"

155

"I missed you," said the woman.

The sea foam bird lowered its head. It spoke but it did not speak. Its word came into their heads like speech, even though it could not form human words.

Human.

"Yes, you are. Again," said the bird.

Bronwyn looked around her. She was standing on the edge of a stream. The hills and forests of her kingdom were gone, only this ordinary forest remained. Her consort was standing next to her. He looked pale and weak; she probably looked the same. His eyes were looking across the stream to something she could not see.

Bronwyn reached out a hand, wanting to brush the hair from his wet forehead. But she stopped herself.

"Agravaine."

He didn't turn toward her.

"He is not yours anymore," said the bird.

Bronwyn closed her eyes while her fingers searched along her abdomen for the wound from the iron sword. Her dress was torn, but the skin was mended by a thick scar.

"Now that the spell is gone and you are whole again, you cannot stay in Illvelion," said the sea foam bird. "That is why you are here, upon these banks."

The bird was a strange mixture of egret, gull, and pelican; its head reached almost to Bronwyn's waist. Its dark eyes looked up into the woman's face, and she stroked its feathered head.

"You came," said Bronwyn. "Must I leave you so soon?"

The bird let out a croak from deep within its throat. "You cannot stay here. You will search for a thousand years and never find Illvelion again. That is the way of it. Depart now with a remembrance of the song we shared. I'm glad you sang to me one last time."

Bronwyn wanted to say something more, to beg forgiveness for what she had considered doing to the sea foam bird. But nothing more needed to be said. It was as if the bird had already known and already forgiven.

The man kept searching the other side of the bank. The sea foam bird turned to him now and spoke to his mind.

"You will not find her there. Go now. Go with the one who can leave. Any path you take will bring you to the edge of the forest. Go. There is much that can be restored if you go."

He didn't answer. What could possibly be restored if his child would not return? He had rather be eaten as food for the fairies. He had rather be dead in the flood.

Bronwyn let her apologies die on her lips, but she reached out and took his hand in hers. Despite his pale skin, his hand was warm. And despite his grief, he let his fingers entwine with hers.

The bird stretched its wings and flapped them to find the wind. It took flight and sailed to the opposite bank.

The man and woman looked at each other with astonishment.

"Bronwyn?" Agravaine looked at her suddenly, remembering.

She couldn't face him.

"Bronwyn, I thought you were dead."

She had been.

"How did you get here?"

She had crossed the edge of the forest, swallowed a spell, and let the old ones bargain with her. She should have listened to the sea foam bird—in that first meeting long ago when she and the bird first sang together—but instead, she built a kingdom. She built a gate of iron, and she built walls, but they were not enough. Even Gallien had warned her. Warnings and warnings, but she heeded none of them.

"I—" Bronwyn began. "My husband, forgive me."

Agravaine brushed away the tear on her cheek. "What is there to forgive? You were dead and now you are alive again."

"But she—"

Agravaine looked back at the stream. The light from the sun was too bright and he saw nothing. He didn't let Bronwyn see his tears.

"The bird said we must leave her. But how can we?" Agravaine asked. He sounded so lost.

Bronwyn let go of his hand and walked toward the sunlight. She wasn't sure what would happen, only that she couldn't bear to return to Estline without her child. Agravaine would waste away with longing if he had to forget his daughter. Bronwyn would not let that happen. She stepped blindly toward the stream, humming the refrain of the bird's ocean song, hoping for some piece of magic to have lingered.

&a.

Gwenhivar saw that she was standing on the edge of a stream, much like the one that led to the glass pool.

"They must leave?"

The bird was silent, but Gwen knew the answer. "Can I go with them?"

"You are the queen of Illvelion. You are once-human but no more."

"Then take the spell out of me."

"The blood sword is gone."

"Can't we make a new one?"

"With what iron would you fashion it?"

Gwen didn't know. She had no iron, and they were far from the gates the old queen had made. What remained of Illvelion anyway? After the old ones were destroyed, they had seen nothing but the sea crashing over everything. Gwen was surprised that the forest behind her even stood.

"You could rebuild your kingdom," said the bird.

"How? I don't know anything. It was the old ones who taught me."

"They used you," the bird corrected her. "The power was your own."

Gwen turned to look at the vast forest at her back. Trees as ancient as stars stretched for miles and miles. "I would not need to make a gate," she said to herself. "There is no one to keep out anymore. Or is there?" She looked at the bird and trembled. How could she—an enchantress with vast powers—suddenly be so afraid? She would have to find a way to banish the child inside herself. She would have to be strong enough to protect herself. There was no one else to do it for her now.

Suddenly the sea foam bird screeched and flapped its wings violently. It snapped its beak at something. Gwen saw a woman standing on the banks of the stream, shielding her face from the bird's assault.

"This is forbidden!" the bird cried. "How can it be?"

Bronwyn didn't know. She had hummed the ocean song and felt a hand guiding her across the water. She thought it was some spell still lingering inside her heart.

Her daughter stood before her, almost a woman grown. Bronwyn wondered how she had missed so much. The enchantress before her was almost a stranger. The gold from her hair was gone, the blue from her eyes as pale as snow. But something in her face reminded Bronwyn of Agravaine, and she tried to smile.

"A hand brought me here," Bronwyn told the bird who still flapped its wings and snapped at her. "I know no more!"

The sea foam bird ruffled its feathers but did not attack. It calmed itself and then sat down on the grassy bank. "Who am I to argue? The forest does what it will," it said, somewhat sulking. It buried its head under its wing.

The woman and child stood very close. Gwen thought she should know this woman, but no name came to her mind.

"You were the queen," she said at last.

"Yes."

"Can you tell me how to build a kingdom?"

"I wouldn't know," the woman replied. "For I have only ever built prisons."

"But you wore a crown. You built the gates. The castle. Everything. You slew the unicorn to keep it."

"I know. I was desperate—" The woman hesitated, afraid to say the words. "Sometimes we hold on to things even when we shouldn't. I had made the castle, conquered the forest, yes. Illvelion was my own to rule and command. I thought it would be enough. But the gates kept me inside as much as they kept the old ones out. I thought it would be enough."

Enough.

The word stung Bronwyn's heart, the heart that was warm and full and beating once more. Enough to help herself forget. Enough to paper over the abandonment of her child. How foolish and cruel it seemed now! What had she wanted that night when she stepped into the forest and left everything behind? At least Gwenhivar and Agravaine had come over the edge to save each other. Bronwyn had not. She had come for other reasons, ones she could not explain. Even to herself.

"Can't you come back with me?" she asked the child.

Gwen didn't know. She wanted to come, but the sea foam bird had said it was impossible. "I still have a spell inside me. Where my heart once was is only emptiness."

"But you remember, don't you? Your father waits for you on the other side."

"I do remember. That's the curious thing. I remember, but I don't remember. I want to find him, but I don't know who he is."

Bronwyn bit her lip and held back more tears. It had been the same with her. She had remembered, even as she had forgotten. All those faerie knights made of flowers and bark? What had they been but an attempt at remembrance? The longer this enchantress stayed in the forest, the harder it would be to remember, but she would still have the desire.

"If only we had the blood sword," the enchantress said.

The sea foam bird kept its head under its wing, but it clucked in irritation.

Bronwyn's hands were empty. She had nothing to give her daughter.

"What about this?" The voice came from the stream.

Crawling up from the edge of the stream was a young puck, sopping wet and holding something that glinted in the sunlight. The sea foam bird stirred and rushed up to block the puck's way, hissing and snapping its beak.

"Wait!" cried the enchantress. "Let him pass!"

The bird obeyed, dipping its slender neck in deference to the new queen.

"You should not be here," said Gwen, studying the puck's face. "I do not recognize you."

The puck looked down, ashamed. "No, you wouldn't. Not this way. I've changed."

Bronwyn knelt to the little puck. "But I know you," she said, lifting his chin and smiling. "Tom. A true friend. Cursed no longer."

"Not so sure about that," replied Tom. "I thought I was cursed before, but now I see differently. Maybe the old form was the true one. This puck skin... I know I ought to stay in the forest, but I'm not so sure. I wonder if it might be possible... If I could go..." He looked at Gwen.

She studied his face. Beneath the long nose like a root and eyes the color of amber, she thought she saw a trace of something familiar.

"I am queen of Illvelion now," she replied. "You

could always stay here with me. I am in need of advisers. Partners."

Tom smiled. She did know him. Gwen nodded slightly and returned his smile, though much more muted. The emptiness still resided within her.

"I'd like that, I would," he said. Then his eyes looked off into the distance. "But..."

"I know what you want," said Gwen. "I want it too. But the bird says it's impossible. We can never leave the forest, just as these humans can never find Illvelion."

"But she came over," protested Tom, looking at Bronwyn.

"Yes, and you helped me," said Bronwyn. "It was your hand that pulled me across the stream."

"I thought you were Gwen," answered Tom.

"How is that possible?" Bronwyn looked at the sea foam bird. "How did I cross over, and why was this puck there?"

The bird ruffled its feathers. "I do not know. Strange and stranger things have happened."

"I wasn't in the stream," said Tom. "I was by the gates, holding on to them."

"The gates were destroyed by the flood," said Gwen.

"No, they held on and so did I." He lifted his palm, and resting there inside it was a shard of deepest gray iron. "Even the waters couldn't destroy them, I suppose. This was in my hand when I could open my eyes again." He turned to Bronwyn. "I didn't know I was holding your hand. Just holding on. Trying to save what I could."

The enchantress looked at the shard of iron in the

puck's hand. Was it enough to make a new sword? Could this cut the spell out of her?

"Can you teach me the song?" Gwen said, looking at her mother. "The one you sang to call the bird and the flood?"

"I—" Bronwyn didn't know if she could. She was an ordinary human again. No more power resided within her except the ordinary power of a woman. "I could try."

The sea foam bird waited, unsure of what would happen next. The human woman shouldn't even be here on this side of the stream.

Bronwyn looked at the bird. "What will happen if I teach her to sing our song? Will you help her make a new sword?"

"I do not know. None of this has happened before."

Bronwyn opened her lips and listened for something resembling the wind. It was too silent here on these placid banks. This was no shoreline where the waves rushed in and out. Could she remember the song without the sea to guide her?

The treetops rustled. At first, a light breeze caught them, then something stronger. A gusting wind came rushing upon them, and the smell of salt air was carried on the wind. Bronwyn heard a note catching in the leaves: a shaking song, a tremulous melody. Then the voice of the sea foam bird drifted into her head and she mimicked it.

"That's a song!" said Tom, jumping. "I hear it! Sing with her, Gwen!"

Gwen tried. She couldn't hear what Tom heard, but she felt something within her breast that seemed to match the woman's voice. Opening her mouth, she began to sing.

The white bird lifted off into the sky. The wind was strong, but the bird's wings buffeted the gale. It began to fly along the stream bank, headlong into the direction of the wind.

Tom and Gwen followed. The wind was like the breath of a storm, but the sun shined above them and no clouds turned gray.

Bronwyn kept singing as long as her lungs would let her, but she could not follow the children. The wind was too strong; her feet were rooted to the place. And soon, when she looked around, the stream was gone. Agravaine was by her side again. They were standing at the edge of the fairies' forest, peering in, seeing nothing but shadows between the trees.

"This is the lawn where last I saw you dance," Agravaine said. "How I wished it had never happened! The fairies put something into the air that night and took you away. I see it now. I thought you had died, but they had bewitched you. And they have taken our Gwen too. We should never have trifled with these dances and fairy games."

Bronwyn shook her head. "It was not the fairies. God forgive me, it was me! My own fault. And still, you must pay for my sins." She buried her head in her hands and wept.

Agravaine wanted to go to her, but he didn't. He felt like a stranger to her.

Bronwyn wanted to go to him, but she didn't. She wept into her hands and wished for a way to turn back time.

They stood there a long time, two strangers, with grieving hearts united.

❧

Tom and Gwen ran along the edge of the stream; the wind blew into their faces like a gale. The sea foam bird was ahead, cutting through the wind like a scythe. The song was still sung, but it was sung above them by the wind, and it was sung below them by the waters, and Gwen willed the song to be sung, while the bird followed it.

The dragonflies buzzed around them and the waters of the stream sparkled. Golden fish leaped from the water as if they were racing Gwen and Tom.

Gwen found herself laughing at the race, and at Tom's nimble feet as he skipped over roots and rocks. All the weight of her power melted away, and for that brief moment, she felt like a child again.

The ground sloped downward and the heavy sound of falling water cut through the wind. The stream emptied into a deep pool.

The trees were now tall and thick and ancient, blocking out the sun. The sea foam bird floated down into the darkened valley and rested by the pool of water. The wind had stopped blowing.

"This is it," said Gwen.

"The glass pool?" answered Tom. "Will it give us the answer? How do we ask?"

Gwen looked at the bird, but its head rested under its wing again. Then she went to the edge of the pool. All was silent except the faint sound of the falling water upstream. The water was as she remembered: as still as glass. She saw her reflection in the pool and did not recognize the young woman looking back. Her hair was almost white and her eyes a dull gray. Her dress was as pale as the moon. She looked like one who could be cruel and terrible.

"Give me the shard," she said to Tom.

He obeyed, careful not to let the sharp edge cut his skin or hers.

Tom needn't have been so careful. With one swift cut, Gwen ran the shard across her palm. Blood dripped into the water, but those few drops did not disturb the pool's stillness.

The edge of the shard dripped with her blood, and before she could think, Gwen tossed it into the placid waters. This time the pool rippled gently as the iron shard sank like a pebble into the depths.

Then the wind cried out, shaking even these trees which were as wide as houses. The sea foam bird jumped up and flapped its wings and flew toward the pool and dove down upon the surface, but its beak hit the water and bounced off. There was a loud crack as the bird's beak broke.

The pool of water had turned to glass.

"No!" cried Gwen, rushing to the bird's side. Its broken beak was splintered where it had been severed. The bird lay on the ground, lifeless, a heap of white feathers.

"No," Gwen repeated, tears starting to fall. She had hardly known this creature, but something about its lifeless body—its fragile neck, its downy feathers —made her abhor such a death. Why had it tried to dive into the water? What was it trying to achieve? She felt it was her fault; it was her selfishness that brought them to this place.

Tom didn't know what to do. He had wanted the

blood sword made too, but not this way. Not this cost. Everything was going all wrong again. He hated himself for it.

Gwen lifted the poor bird's body and tried to will it back to life. She was the enchantress, after all, the new queen of Illvelion. But the song barely croaked from her lips. All melodies were forgotten.

Tom came to her side. Together they laid the bird's body softly down.

"We shouldn't have come," Gwen said.

"No, we should've left well enough alone. Been satisfied with our lot."

Both of them sat silently for a long while.

At last, Gwen spoke. "What was it trying to do? What was it trying to get?"

Tom stood up and went to the edge of the glass pool. There below the surface was a slender sword, dark as iron

Gwen saw it too. She took hold of Tom's hand.

"Would this be like the other one?" she asked. "The one that released the spell from the queen and her consort?"

"Perhaps," Tom answered.

Gwen stared at the frozen waters. What could they do to break the surface? It looked too thick to break, even if they had some means to do it. The white bird had broken its neck trying to crack that glass.

"Maybe a stone," said Tom. But when he looked around the glade there were no rocks of any kind. Perhaps if they went further up the stream...

"Wait—" Gwen had glanced around too, but her eyes fell unwillingly on the body of the white bird. She tried to look away, but surprise stopped her.

The bird had changed. The feathers were puffy and rounded now; they bubbled like froth at the bottom of a waterfall.

Like sea foam.

Then, from out of the frothing foam, two nostrils emerged as if they were sprouting from the sea. Then a head, shimmering white. Then two eyes and a mane like sea foam and a golden horn that glittered brighter than the sun.

Gallien stood before them, tail flicking back and forth, eyes staring down at their pale faces.

He walked to the edge of the glass pool. Both children wanted to ask how such a thing was possible. But they didn't dare. It was enough that he was here again.

"If you are to break the spell," Gallien said, "you must tell the truth. That is why I came. To hear the truth and to fulfill it."

At first, neither Gwen nor Tom knew what to say.

Then Tom stepped forward. He felt something bubbling up inside. "I want to lift my curse," he said. "That's the truth of it."

"But your curse has been lifted, little puck," replied Gallien. "You are yourself again."

"No," said Tom, shaking his head. "No. I am cursed. I want to break it and be myself again."

Gallien took a step toward him. The unicorn towered over Tom. "And who are you?"

"I am Tom." He looked at Gwen. "And Tom's a human name."

Gallien didn't move. He stared into Tom's eyes, searching the puck's face for the truth. "Do you know what that would mean?"

"I'd have to leave this place," answered Tom.

"But that's okay. Because then I could go with her." He smiled at Gwen, his cheeks blushing.

"But she cannot go," said Gallien. "Not while the spell resides within her breast."

"Then tell the truth, Gwen," said Tom. "Tell him what you want and we can break the spell!"

Now Gallien's eyes turned to her, but Gwen could not face them. Long ago, she had wanted to find her father, and then she had wanted to find Tom, and then she had wanted other things, terrible things, things she could not name.

She had gotten those terrible things. She had become the queen of Illvelion. What more did she want?

"I want—"

"Go on, Gwen, tell him," said Tom, holding her hand again. "He wants to hear the truth."

"I want—"

"You do not know?" Gallien asked. "You hesitate."

"Tell him, Gwen."

"I—"

Everything was slipping away. Gwen couldn't say the words.

"The glass will not break. You will be doomed to stay," said Gallien.

"Gwen, please!" cried Tom.

Gwen couldn't say the words. She couldn't remember them. She clasped both of Tom's hands. "Will you stay with me? Help me find my way?"

"I won't be human then," Tom answered.

Gwen could hear the disappointment in his voice.

"But I suppose I could..." Tom's face was pale even as he tried to smile.

The words came to her lips unbidden. She said them even though she didn't want to, but something broke the seal of her silence and the words came.

Gwen said, "I'm afraid to be alone."

A wind swirled. Gallien reared up on his hind legs and then came down upon the surface of the pool, his hooves crushing the glass into infinite shards.

The two children shielded their eyes from the flying glass, but when Tom peeked out, he saw the hole in the ground where the glass pool had been and the iron sword exposed.

In a rush, he grabbed for the sword and held it up high. Gwen looked on, trembling.

But Gallien was gone. The forest was still and quiet once more.

"Do we?" Tom said, bringing the sword down and holding its point down awkwardly.

The realization of what they must do hit them at once.

"I couldn't do it," said Gwen. "Even if you held it in front of me. I couldn't run upon it."

"Nay, me neither."

"Then all this for nothing."

"Not nothing," said Tom. He laid the sword down on the dirt and leaves. "You don't have to fear no longer." He took her hand in his and held it tightly. "You're not alone."

His skin was rough like sandpaper, and his eyes were two amber oil lamps of light. But beneath the crooked face and root-like nose, Gwen saw something of the human boy she first beheld in these woods.

"I wish I knew the way back to the gates," she

said. "They are as good a place as any to rebuild my stronghold."

"I could try to remember," said Tom. "I found my way there once, trying to save you. I thought so anyway. But I guess you didn't need saving."

"No, I was the threat, wasn't I?"

"Only 'cause the old ones made you."

"I did need saving, then. You weren't wrong."

"Nay, not wrong. But not much use either."

Gwen laughed. "How wrong you are, Tom! You saved us all! You, standing there with Gallien's horn. You fought the old ones for me."

"Aye and got myself hacked to death in the process."

"It was enough. It was what—"

"—cut the curse out of me. Only I wish it hadn't. That other face—that human one—I think that was the true face."

"What of my face?" said Gwen, solemnly. "Is this pale, faded face my true one?"

Tom didn't know. It was true that the Gwen standing beside him was very different from the young girl he had first met in the forest.

"Ah well," sighed Gwen. "No use dwelling. Let us away upstream and try to find the gates."

She started to go, but Tom tugged the hem of her dress and silently motioned in the other direction. They both looked at a huge shape of leaves and mud trudging along in the distance.

"Gallien again? But it can't be..." said Tom.

"No. Wherever he's gone, I don't think he'll come back," answered Gwen. "But I know that shape. I've seen it before." She took a step toward the shuffling mass. "Come on."

Tom followed, and for some reason, he reached down and took hold of the sword again. He could never use it against Gwen or himself, but that didn't mean he could never use it. Something about that leafy mass made him uneasy.

"Not too close," whispered Gwen. She too felt the unease.

The shuffling mound meandered through the darkening wood. The further and further it went, the thicker the trees became, until all traces of the sun were blotted out by the foliage. Still, the shuffling mass kept up its wandering, first to the north, then to the south, then backtracked to the east, and then forward to the west again. The children had to be careful not to let it see them when it retraced its steps.

"Do you think it's looking for something in particular?" Tom managed to whisper as quietly as he could.

"I don't know," said Gwen. "But something about it is familiar."

Tom lifted the sword and pointed it for protection. Gwen had her magic, but there's nothing a fairy hated more than cold iron.

"Wait," said Gwen, and she held up a hand to stop them both. "Look."

The creature was stopped now too and rummaging around in the underbrush. It was mumbling to itself.

"'Tis not the way, no how. All befuddled I am. Where the wind blows and here I am lost as a porcupine in daylight."

The heap of a creature sat down then in a huff, and reached inside its mass of leaves and twigs and pulled out a telescope.

"Hide!" Gwen cried in a hoarse whisper, for she could see that the creature would soon turn its spyglass on them. She shoved Tom toward a batch of brambles.

But it was too late.

"What's this, eh?" called the creature. "Two fairies come to bother an old hag? Come out ye rascals! Come out and get an earful from an old wretch who shouldn't be bothered with yer spying!"

"Remember," said Tom in a low voice, "you are the queen after all. Don't let that thing boss you around."

Gwen was the queen, so she stood up as regally as she could and walked out from the brambles. As she drew closer to the creature, she realized what it was.

"I knows ye!" said Troll-Hag with a laugh. "The little girl who lost her father! Not so little no more, I'd wager. My spell's done good work."

Gwen glared at her. "Take the spell out," she commanded. "As your sovereign queen, I demand it."

"Queen, eh? So ye gave up on yer father, did ye? All's well then, as they say. Bet ye could crush ol' Troll-Hag with one wave of yer finger, as it were. And ye'll have to. A heart wrought with spells cannot be unwrought."

"You're wrong," said Tom, coming up behind Gwen. "This blood sword could do it. We've seen it done!"

"Then use yer blood sword yerself," spat Troll-Hag. "I ain't having no part in it."

"You will," said Gwen, her face as hard as stone. "Take this sword, and with it, make another one of your draughts. Something to kill the spell."

"And yerselves too," chuckled Troll-Hag. "I swear ol' Troll-Hag can't wrap her head around you humans and near-humans and once-humans. All as looney as the moon!"

"I didn't ask for you to understand, just to obey."

Shaking her head and lifting her great girth off the ground, Troll-Hag reached out and wrenched the sword from Tom's hand.

He was loathe to let it go, but Troll-Hag's strength was too much for him.

"Can't make no draught if we can't find my hovel," said Troll-Hag. "All my wares are there, after all."

"You're lost?" said Gwen."

"Aye, as lost as a blind rat."

"Rats can smell to find their way," said Tom.

"Can they now? Well, 'tis time I found better sayings! No matter, though. I'm still lost."

"You don't need your hovel," said Gwen. "I know another cauldron."

ॐ

With a rock, Troll-Hag scraped flecks of iron into the glass pool. Water from the stream had flowed into it again forming a puddle at the bottom. When she was done scraping, Troll-Hag tossed the sword away like an old bone. Then, with her thick, muddy finger, she stirred the puddle of water and muttered under her breath.

"There," she said, standing straight again and coming up out of the pool. "'Tis done. Yer spell. Though I 'spose 'tis not a spell so much as the end of one. Well, no matter."

"We must drink it," Gwen told Tom.

"Can it be that simple?" replied Tom. "I thought the sword had to cut the magic out of us."

"Who's to say it won't? We haven't drunk yet."

Troll-Hag began to hum a strange tune as she shuffled along. She had left the children behind and went looking for her hovel again.

Gwen and Tom stood above the puddle, their fingers entwined.

"Together," Gwen said.

"Together."

The water was cool on their lips, its flavor a metallic tang. They lay down beside each other in the hole in the ground that was once the glass pool and felt their throats tighten. The iron choked them. They coughed and gasped, but never did they let go of the other's hand. They lay together as they struggled to breathe, and Gwen knew that Tom had changed. His skin was no longer rough like sand, his fingers were slender again. When Gwen opened her eyes, she saw a familiar face.

"I know you," she said, barely able to exhale the words.

"And I you." Tom smiled right before he closed his eyes. Gwen's hair was the color of Gallien's horn and her eyes as bright as stars.

They felt the warmth of each other. They heard the slow beating of their hearts. They closed their eyes and dreamed.

EPILOGUE

The lawn was dry from the heat of the day. A blanket of the richest purple lay upon it, and the lord and lady of Estline reclined there.

It was almost twilight, but the lawn was quiet, except for the buzzing of stray bumblebees, and the large dragonflies who flitted around in circles near the tops of the trees.

The lord had brought a simple supper to the lawn, two or three wicker baskets of bread and summer berries and honey.

He smiled at his wife, hoping that she would smile back. But the lady's face was grave—as it always was—and lost in thoughts deep and dark. Her eyes went sometimes to the edge of the woods, but she never let them linger there.

The lord did not press her. He was patient.

After a short while, the lady turned and saw his shining eyes and gave him a fleeting smile. It was swift but true.

They took to eating and watched the fireflies begin to light.

No one else was on the lawn but they two and the rising moon.

"Are you sure you want to do this?" Lord Agravaine asked.

The lady Bronwyn nodded.

After they finished their meal, they stood and cleared away the blanket and food. There were no drummers or pipers or revelers. No music. Only the lord and his lady. Alone upon the lawn.

Lord Agravaine clasped his wife's hand and felt the band of her sapphire ring against his finger. They bowed to each other.

Then they began to dance.

Bronwyn danced with wild abandon, with all her heart. She spun and spun, and swirled with Agravaine, hand in hand.

"Do they see us?" Bronwyn cried. "Do they approve?"

Agravaine couldn't answer. Despite the movements of his body, his mind was unconvinced. How many nights had they come here and danced and still no sign from the forest? He could not dance as she did.

"We must go nearer!" the lady shouted.

But Agravaine shook his head. No, they could not go too near the edge. He feared that he would lose her again. He hated himself for being afraid, for not going back into the forest for his child, but the way back was too evil, a trap from which none of them would escape.

So they danced, and Bronwyn hoped. *Maybe this night would be the night,* she thought. *Maybe this time they will see.*

"You must hold nothing back!" Bronwyn cried to

her husband. "Please!"

Agravaine tried. He tried to let every part of himself flow into the dance. But he could not.

"Please, my love! Please!" Bronwyn gripped his hands tighter as they spun. Her heart was bursting with longing, with sorrow, with hope.

Agravaine saw the pain in his wife's eyes. If only he could heal it... If only he had healed it before... If only...

Why do I hold back? he wondered. *What am I afraid of?*

Asking the question was like breaking the spell. It was like a star falling from the sky. Like a blaze of light and sparks everywhere. It was a kind of heat that Agravaine had never felt before. Something inside him burst.

For the first time in his life, Agravaine gave himself entirely to the dance. He and his wife were as one. He didn't know if the fairies could see, or his child, or if anything lay past the edge of that forest, but he danced as if the queen of Illvelion herself was watching.

He wept as he danced, and he smiled, and together he and Bronwyn laughed, a laughter full of mirth and joy and hope.

"Look!" she cried. "A gull!"

Above them, strange against the rising moon, was the silhouette of a seagull, gliding over the lawn and heading toward the west.

Agravaine hoped. Perhaps it was a sign.

At last, their energy gave out. They collapsed in exhaustion. Everything was still and silent.

They waited. Their eyes searched the edge of the trees.

They waited long into the night.

There was nothing.

No sign.

Without a word to each other, the lord and lady gathered up their things and made their way back to the manor house. The disappointment they felt went unspoken between them. Could they keep enough hope alive till the next full moon?

"I thought it was a sign," Bronwyn said under her breath. That white gull had seemed to mean something. But it was just an ordinary bird.

"I did too," Agravaine answered. He had let his heart believe—had let down all his guard—but it was for naught. The crushing weight of his disappointment could not be measured.

When the humans were gone, the lawn sat empty. Even the fireflies had abandoned it. No wind stirred the air that night. The moon was so bright it outshone the stars.

From the edge of the woods, two faces watched the stillness.

"Should we go?" said the first face.

"Fearsome things are past the edge of the forest," said the second face.

"Yes. But they danced so well."

"They did. With all their hearts."

"Come on. Let's follow."

The lord and lady of Estline had gone up the hill, back to their manor. They did not see two creatures creep out of the forest and follow after them.

One a head of sandy hair and one a head of gold. A sapphire dress torn at the hem. Bare feet covered in dirt.

Two human faces, eager for the warmth of home.

ABOUT THE AUTHOR

A.R. Rathmann is the author of such fantasy gems as *Hobart's Gambit*, *The Bone Breakers*, and *Zazamaz the Arcane*.